RIVALS

Book 2 of
THE WARDEN

FELICIA JEDLICKA

SISTER WITCHES
THE DEVIL'S SHADOW
THE DEVIL'S SOUL

DESTINY REJECTED
DESTINY RECLAIMED
DESTINY RAZED
DESTINY RESTORED

DÉJÀ VU

SAVE THE HUMANS

THE NECROMANCER'S CHILD

<u>**THE NEBRASKA APOCALYPSE NOVELS**</u>
CORN COWS AND THE APOCALYPSE
COW TIPPING AFTER THE APOCALYPSE
CORN HUSKING AFTER THE APOCALYPSE

<u>**THE WARDEN SERIES**</u>
SUCCESSORS
RIVALS
LOVERS AND LIARS
BAD BLOOD
TENANTS AND TYRANTS
THE RING BEARER
GODS AND MONSTERS
BEASTS AND BURDENS
MAGIC AND MAYHEM
FORK IN THE ROAD
DETAILS AND DEADLINES
*CURSES AND SACRIFICES**
*WITCHES AND WOLVES**
*SAINTS AND SERPENTS**
*ENEMIES AND ALLIES**

MARRIED TO DEATH*

Rivals

Felicia Jedlicka

1

CORI SPRINTED DOWN THE hall of the zoological floor. Her lungs burned, and her side ached, but she was ahead of Ethan, so she ignored the pain. She glanced back at him. Despite the three-foot-long harpoon gun he was carrying, he was closing the distance between them. She had opted for a more civilized weapon. A tranquilizer gun wasn't as effective in these situations, but it was a lot easier to carry.

At the end of the hall, the elevator doors opened unexpectedly. Seeing an opportunity to extend her lead, Cori lengthened her strides to a hamstring-tearing pace.

"Don't you dare," Ethan snarled from behind her, already anticipating her plan.

Reaching the elevator at full speed, she crashed into the back wall less than gracefully. She leaped back to the panel, nearly toppling against it as she pressed the "door close" button.

The doors began to shut.

She heard Ethan roar, and he leaped through the gap in the closing doors. He collided with the back wall before dropping to a heap on the floor. Even with the double impact, he kept his gargantuan harpoon gun in his hand. He glowered at her from the floor, panting his exertion through flaring nostrils.

Cori pinched back her smile and positioned herself in front of the door. He joined her, all but shoving her aside to get equal access to it.

They silently watched the dial over the door that indicated the car's slow ascension. The half clock was virtually useless since most of the numbers had fallen off. All the elevators were in sad order, and she was certain that one day someone might plummet to their death in one. She was just hoping not to be that someone.

While they were waiting, she checked her tranquilizer gun, ensuring it was still securely attached to her belt. Ethan put down the harpoon to tuck his black shirt into his black cargo pants. She wanted to mock him about his monochromatic military style, but the truth was he looked good in the uniform.

She still donned her usual jeans and graphic t-shirt. Today's wardrobe choice depicted a man sitting on a toilet with a big smile and a double thumbs-up. It read, "Pooping is Fun!" The shirt had inspired looks of disgust from Danato, which made it her favorite.

There had technically been no formal discussion on the dress code, so she took advantage of it. It was her last vestige of rebellion. That was probably why Danato let her do it. Control of her clothing was the least he could do to appease her need for individuality.

In the closed space of the elevator, Cori became acutely aware of the smell of cologne. She looked up at Ethan, wondering when he had become one of those guys. His jaw clenched, as if preparing for her verbal attack. Instead of taking the opening to tease him, she grazed her eyes along the taut muscles of his neck and down to the sculpted chest that was panting from his exertion.

He's dead.

The reminder snapped Cori away from her appreciative ogling. She shouldn't have been gawking at him like that, anyway. He was too young—not as young as he had been, but of course, neither was she. Perhaps it wasn't so much about him being too young anymore, as her being too old.

He's dead.

Cori shook her head, clearing away the etch-a-sketch. Ethan noted the oddity of the movement and leaned forward to see her face. When nothing revealed itself to him, he went back to staring at the dial. "What are you making for dinner tonight?" he asked.

"Stroganoff," she answered.

"I love stroganoff."

"I know," she answered with a hint of pride for the knowledge.

He looked down at her, eyes fluttering over her with awe. She smirked at his enthusiasm. It was the simple things that struck Ethan's heart. She imagined that his on-again-off-again foster care had left him longing for home-cooked meals.

A slight smile perched on his lips, and his eyes softened. For a moment, she thought he might hug her or kiss her, but he didn't have a chance to do either.

The doors opened with a *ponk* at the seducers' level. Game on.

Cori lunged forward to take the lead again, but Ethan shoved her to one side before she could even get out of the lift. Her intended momentum redirected her face first into the button console.

"Damn you!" she griped, but he was long gone.

Several floors had been selected, courtesy of her forehead, and the doors started to close again. She slipped between them, but her foot got caught up. Fearful that the antiquated device would cut off her foot, she yanked herself free, minus her shoe. "Son of a..." she muttered, ripping off her sock.

She looked down the corridor. Ethan had already made it into the next section. She screamed in frustration and ran after him.

When Cori reached the first airlock, she discovered the glass in the door was broken. The end result of an escapee with a hard head and no opposable thumbs—or hands.

She tiptoed through the sharp mine field to the door. She considered simply stepping through the vacancy, but the jagged remnants lining the doorframe left it too narrow to pass through without getting cut. Despite the obvious section breach, the system still insisted she close the previous door before opening the next.

When she finally caught up with Ethan and their escape artist, he was already hauling the screeching creature down from the ceiling. Even with the harpoon pierced through the wing of the small pterodactyl-like creature, it was still trying to fly away. It took everything Ethan had to draw the creature down to him.

Though it wasn't inherently violent, it was extremely dangerous. Its knobby head and jet speed designed it to be an airborne battering ram. If it turned on Ethan, he would be the recipient of a skull-crushing head butt.

When it finally flopped to the floor, Ethan used the remainder of his rope to hogtie the beast. It squawked and flailed in objection, but he quickly wove it into a tight bundle, not much larger than a bulldog. Once it was calm, the creature turned to look at Cori. She wasn't sure the elongated beak could project a pout, but it was definitely unhappy to be denied the expanse of the prison as a playground.

Ethan panted over his prey with his arms on his hips. When he noticed her, he frowned. "Where the bloody hell have you been?" he barked.

Her mouth fell open, and she pointed back to the endless sea of glass that had threatened to shred her naked foot. Before she could articulate her explanation, she noticed the amusement trickling into his smile.

She glowered at his teasing, and he outright grinned at her. She growled through clenched teeth and stalked past him.

"What happened to your shoe?" he scoffed behind her.

"Shut up!" she yelled back at him as she left the section. She heard the beginnings of his hearty guffaws before she shut the door to the airlock.

2

CORI STORMED INTO THE house and slammed the door behind her. She ripped off her coat and slapped it over the back of the couch. Danato eyeballed the misplaced coat over the rim of his glasses from his usual reading chair. "I can't believe you," she bristled as Ethan came in behind her. He closed the door gently and rubbed the frame as if he was concerned that she had damaged it with her pubescent spectacle.

"Did you get the buzzard?" Danato asked.

Ethan nodded and hung his coat up. "Yes, we did," he said with a restrained smile.

"*He* got it!" Cori tattled to Danato. "Even after he specifically said *I* could take it down." She stormed past Ethan, clipping his shoulder with hers on the way by. He grunted from the abuse, but she assumed it was just to mock her further.

"Do you not remember saying that?" she asked, searching the cupboards for food. Stroganoff was off the menu for the evening. Since it was his favorite, she considered it his punishment for not upholding his deal.

"I do remember that." Ethan picked up her coat from the couch and hung it up by the door. "Imagine how disappointed I was to find out it wasn't true."

Cori paused with a soda and chips in hand to grasp his meaning. "So clever," she hissed and headed upstairs.

"Don't take all the chips. That's the last bag until next week," Ethan demanded with a fatherly scold.

She turned around and stuck her tongue out at him with a childish sass. She expected him to threaten her verbally, but she hadn't anticipated him launching into a dead sprint to get to her. She yelped and ran up the stairs, no longer concerned for chips or soda, but for the safety of her body.

He tackled her midway up and ripped the bag from her grip. Uninterested in retaliation beyond taking another prize from her, he continued up the stairs. She grabbed for his feet, but he hopped away from her grasp and disappeared into his room.

"Ethan. Give them back!" Unwilling to relinquish any more to him, she got to her feet—soda forgotten—and ran to his door. She pounded on the thick wood. "Open this door or I'll beat it down! You know I will."

She backed up; giving herself the running start she needed for a truly dramatic entrance. She ran to the door and leaped into it with her shoulder. With prolonged airtime, and a far greater impact than she'd expected, she reached her ultimate destination: the floor inside the room.

Ethan closed the unharmed door behind her, shaking his head. "Don't wreck the house; she's already miffed at you."

Cori took in a few whistling inhalations, forcing air back into her vacant lungs. She rolled over and found the chips. She grabbed the foil bag, but it was a short-lived triumph.

Empty. Wrong bag. *Damn.*

"Looking for this one?" Ethan flaunted the full bag of chips over her before ensconcing himself on a black leather couch. His monochromatic style had officially reached the point of excess.

While he devoured the contents of the bag, Cori examined her surroundings. She was in a bachelor's living room. Modern white plastic end tables surrounded the black leather couch. Books and a few trinkets filled the bookshelves lining the walls. The room even smelled musky, like his cologne.

"Where's your bed?" she asked, searching the walls for a hide-away bed.

"In the bedroom," he mumbled over his chips. He motioned to the door behind her on the left.

"What?" She backed up and peeked into the fully furnished bedroom. The black embellishments continued, making the room seem dark. "You expanded into the spare bedroom," she said, probing deeper into his personal space. She found a rather impressive bathroom and a walk-in closet. "I can't believe I didn't notice this. When did you guys redo the house?" she yelled from the closet.

"The house redid herself," Ethan hollered from the living room. "She decides how much room you need."

"Your closet is bigger than my bathroom." She emerged from the bedroom and glared at him with pouty lips.

"The house likes me. She doesn't like you."

"What the hell did I ever do to her?" she shrilled.

"Besides that little stunt you *almost* just pulled." He nodded to the door.

"What?" She shrugged and moved to the couch. "I didn't hurt anything." Cori crouched on the cushion next to him.

"Hey, shoes off or sit right," he said, pointing to her scruffy tennis shoes on his fine leather. Cori rolled her eyes. She was amazed at how quickly he had adapted to and adopted Danato's OCD cleanliness. "You are disorganized and messy. You punched a hole in her wall."

"I never did that," Cori objected as she slipped her tennis shoes off and tossed them to the floor.

"The first night you were here, you punched a hole in the office wall. It made an impression on her."

"Oh!" She thought about that a moment while she repositioned herself to sit Indian style on the couch. "I didn't know the house could... Did that hurt her?" she asked, suddenly concerned about every supposedly harmless act of violence against inanimate objects in the house.

"I'm not sure it was physically painful," Ethan said. "But she is a very emotional being. I think you hurt her feelings."

"Oh." She thought about that. "Can she hear us?" Cori whispered.

Ethan laughed. "No, she's just a presence. If the house is clean and in good order, she is happy. If not, the degree of sloppiness will determine if she's sad or mad."

"So, to get my room expanded, I have to clean it."

"Yup." Ethan nodded. "Show appreciation for what she has offered you."

With a quick movement, Cori grabbed the chips and ran to the door. Ever prepared for her tactical maneuvers, Ethan tackled her before she could reach the door. The bag of chips landed beneath them both with a devastating crunch. "You smashed them!" she yelled.

"I did? You're on top of them," Ethan protested.

"And you're on top of me. Ergo, get off me!"

Ethan rolled off her. Cori rolled off the bag of chips. They examined the downed comrade between them with disappointment.

Cori got up and dusted herself off. "You can have them."

"Not hungry anymore?" Ethan asked.

"Yeah, but without the crunch, what's the point?" Cori shrugged and left.

She went to her bedroom to prepare for bed. She grabbed her pajamas and slipped out of her t-shirt and jeans. As usual, she tossed them on the floor, nowhere near the hamper, and slipped on her pajamas.

She looked down at the discarded clothes. Determined to turn over a new leaf of order and cleanliness, she picked them up to place them in the bathroom hamper. As she did, she noticed a red stain on the back of her shirt. It looked like blood.

"Shit." She ran to her bathroom mirror to check her back for cuts, but there wasn't a scratch on her. She quickly retraced her steps and realized that she wasn't the source of the blood. "Idiot!" she hissed.

She reached below the sink and found her handy-dandy first aid kit. After several trips to the infirmary, it was clear more paperwork was involved in getting hurt than dying. Therefore, unless you are dying, you don't go to the infirmary. To save a few trees, and her sanity, she kept a few basic supplies at home. In case she had any incidents.

Cori stepped back across the hall and found her shoes just outside Ethan's door. She knocked. "Look down," he voiced from inside.

"Open up," she said quietly, so she didn't disturb Danato any further than they already had. It surprised her he hadn't come upstairs to break up their scuffle. He didn't like it when they got into physical fights. Danato knew better than anyone how strong Ethan was, and if he didn't restrain himself in their playful banters, he could really hurt her. So far, he hadn't. Since this was only one of a series of fights they had been having the last few weeks, Danato was probably sick of intervening.

"You can't have the chips," he said, muffled by the door and the handful of chips he most likely just put in his mouth.

"Open up or I'll tell Danato you need to go to the infirmary." A moment later, the door unlatched and opened a crack. Ethan peeked out with one glaring eye. The other eye was likely glaring too, but she could only see the one. "I know you're hurt," she said, using her maternal voice: a combination of sweetness, and *don't make me come in there.*

"I'm fine."

"As soon as I determine that for myself, then we can both go on with our lives." After a long pause with no response, Cori opened her mouth to holler downstairs to Danato. Ethan opened the door wide and yanked her inside.

She chuckled at their common hatred of infirmary paperwork as she put her kit down on the end table. She opened it to reveal a plethora of stolen medical supplies. She even had syringes. Yes, she was willing to inject herself with sharp, pointy metal to avoid paperwork. Apparently, Ethan felt the same way.

He studied her stash while he crunched on chip debris.

"Take your shirt off," she requested and turned to see a rather devious smile on his face.

"Don't you want to take it off for me?" He perked his brow. She didn't rise to his baiting. Instead, she gave him her maternal stare: a combination of compassion; and *do you really want to mess with me?* He groaned and sat down on the couch. "Can't you just leave me the box?"

"If it's not that bad, you can do it yourself. Take your shirt off. I do have sedatives in here."

With another grumble that turned into a hiss, he removed the black t-shirt, which didn't appear ripped, but she could tell now that the moisture she had earlier mistaken for sweat was actually blood. A long gash crossed his sternum high on his chest. "Damn it, Ethan." She couldn't help but whine. The cut was deep enough that she considered braving the paperwork.

"What?" he asked with ignorance to her vexation.

"What?" she mocked. "You need stitches for that."

"How can you tell?" He looked down.

"I can see bone, dipshit." She shook her head as she gathered her items. After sterilizing her needle and thread, she brought the alcohol to him. He shook his head with the grimace of a child refusing to take his medicine even before the spoon was offered. "Don't be a baby; sit on your hands so you're not tempted to defend yourself."

He groaned and sat on his hands. She looked around him, trying to figure out how she should position herself to do her work.

Ethan laughed at her. "Oh, just straddle me. You know it's easier."

"Yeah, yeah, try to keep your comments to yourself."

"It won't be my comments–" He stopped short and shook his head, refusing to say more.

"Thank you." She straddled him as he had suggested and used his shirt to catch the excess alcohol so it didn't get on the couch. "You went through the glass in the airlock doors, didn't you? That's how you got ahead of me so fast."

"Yeah."

"All that just to beat me?"

His face crinkled with confusion. "No, all that for the job. If I slowed down every time I might get hurt, I'd be at a full stop before I started."

She poured the liquid pain onto his wound and his head bucked back. His neck muscles contracted as he clenched his jaw. She poured again. He growled, but released his jaw. On the third splash, he could bring his head back to face her.

She sewed together the biggest part of the laceration to get the tissue aligned. As she focused on her medical work, she felt him watching her with the same intensity. She pressed on his chest each time she needed to suture the cut. She could feel his heart pounding against her fingers. He was warm, too. She wasn't sure why that surprised her, but it did. She could feel his sinewy muscle under smooth, soft skin. The muscles that she had been eyeing appreciatively earlier that day.

He's dead.

She shook the harsh reality from her mind.

"What's wrong?" Ethan asked softly. "Why do you keep doing that?"

She looked at him. "It's nothing. I just have this thought that keeps rattling in my head. I'm trying not to let it interfere with my life, but it just pops in there."

"What thought?"

Cori's face melted, and she broke eye contact. "Vince," she whispered, almost ashamed to bring it up to him. She knew Ethan resented everything about Vince and her time with him, so she tried not to broach the subject around him.

Even Danato tiptoed around the topic. She wasn't sure if it was for her sake or Ethan's, but either way, Danato didn't express sentiment well. He was a teddy bear with the emphasis on *bear*.

"That sounds like a reasonable topic to have rattling around in your head. You sound embarrassed by it."

Cori scoffed as she motioned to their position. "I'm ashamed because I'm straddling a half-naked man on his couch. I don't know if I feel guilty because I'm here with you thinking of him, or..." Whatever amusement she found in the situation was lost. "...or because I'm here with you, *not* thinking of him."

Ethan pulled his hands free and rubbed her arms. "We're not doing anything wrong, Cori. You have nothing to be ashamed of."

She wasn't sure he would say that if he knew what thoughts had prompted the reminder. "I feel sad when I think about him, and I feel guilty when I don't think about him, but I feel like a complete jerk when I think about other... futures without him." Translation: she felt like a tramp when she admired another man when Vince had only died a few months ago.

Ethan squeezed her arms. "You will have a future without him. That is inevitable. I know everyone always says that 'he would want you to be happy,' but the bottom line is, he is no longer here to induce your happiness."

He's dead.

Ethan dragged his hands down her arms to rest against her hips. "When my parents died, I shoved a lot of people away, because I thought they were trying to replace them. I didn't want anyone to replace my parents. Unfortunately, I pushed too hard for too long, and I lost out on a lot of opportunities to be part of a family. I regret it, but I wouldn't change a single day if it meant losing you."

Cori swallowed hard at that declaration.

"Or Danato," he added. "I just mean, this is my home now."

She nodded and looked down at the intimate positions of their bodies. "How do we do this?"

"What?" Ethan's eyes bulged from his head.

"We start the day off screaming at each other, then we end up in a pseudo psychiatric session with stitches."

He shrugged. "We just haven't figured out our rhythm yet. Maybe someday we'll find a better way to release all that pent-up rage." She smiled, catching his eyes with a meaningful glance.

He was right. They *were* family. She had refused to see it while she was still pining for her freedom, but now, in the wake of tragedy, it was more evident. Ethan was loyal and gentle, despite what their bickering brought out in him. She cared for him a good deal, but lately she wasn't sure how to define those feelings.

Ethan flinched under her examination and broke the connection prematurely. "I'm going to finish up these stitches." He took the needle from her. "Why don't you head to bed?"

"I..." She struggled to counter his dismissal. She wasn't really ready to be done with the conversation. It was a rare thing for them to converse without arguing. "What did I say?"

He stood up with her still on his lap. He braced her back with a strong arm and let her slide down his body until her feet touched the floor.

"Nothing. It's fine. You worked hard today, get some rest. Thank you for the medical care." He gave her a quick, almost jolting kiss on the cheek before breaking away from her. He disappeared into his bedroom with the needle and a bottle of alcohol.

She wanted to follow him in, to find out what was bothering him, but she decided there could be any number of things bothering him at that point: their almost intimate situation, her ill-timed confession of guilt about her ex. If he had something to say to her, it was unlikely that he would keep it hidden for long.

Instead, she went to bed, with only one thought rolling around in her head.

He's dead.

T HE NEXT MORNING, DANATO poured himself a big
bowl of muesli at the dining room table. He had
missed the memo the night before about dinner being
canceled, so he had gone to bed hungry. Ethan and Cori
were finding their own breakfasts as well.

Their arguing was becoming problematic—especially
since it was affecting his meals. He knew they needed time
to figure each other out. He wanted to give them the space
to do that, but he didn't like that it was taking so long.

Ethan was on the defensive for his job, and Cori was on
the offensive for her pride. The fact that Ethan was head
over heels in love with her was only adding to the tension.
If Cori hadn't just lost her lover, they might have had a
shot at an honest flirtation, but as it was now, they were
both dancing around their emotions. The result was weeks
upon weeks of bitching and bickering about anything and
everything other than their true feelings.

Cori opened the upper cabinet in search of cereal.
Ethan came in behind her and grabbed the chocolate puff

cereal that was just out of her reach. "Ethan, there's only enough for one bowl in there."

"So, I'll have some fruit with it." He grabbed a bowl and spoon.

"You ate the first five bowls. I want the last bowl."

"How does the cereal that I requisition have your name on the last bowl?" He gestured at her with the box.

"Because you ate the chips I requisitioned last night. I want my peace offering in the form of chocolate, and your cereal will do nicely," she said with restrained anger.

"I'll give you this if you make stroganoff tonight."

"Tonight is your night," she corrected.

"You didn't even cook last night!" Ethan yelled.

"Enough!" Danato slammed the table, knocking his spoon from his bowl. It *was* enough. He had stayed out of the way long enough. The rent on *space to figure things out* just went up.

They both gaped at him, presumably oblivious to the cause of his displeasure. "Breakfast is over. Come with me." Danato grabbed his coat and opened the door. The frosty morning breeze wasn't nearly as cold as the glare he offered them when they didn't rush to follow him.

Ethan put down his box and grabbed his coat. He threw Cori hers.

Danato led them out of the house, leaving his second meal in twenty-four hours behind.

Something he never did.

C ORI FOLLOWED DANATO WITHOUT objection. Ethan seemed irritated by the situation, but he didn't object. Inside the prison, they dropped off their coats and went straight to the elevator. Danato pushed the button second from the top.

Ethan seemed to glean understanding after the selection was made. The worried look that crossed his face was there and gone, replaced by a glower that should have been the herald of swear words, but he didn't voice his discontentment.

Cori had never been to the sixth floor, so she had no reason to complain, but she didn't like that Ethan was so unhappy with the choice. She glanced between the two men, but neither looked her way. The silent argument kept them more than occupied.

The elevator opened, and they stepped into the vestibule. The only option to proceed was a set of heavy metal doors that gated off the remainder of the floor. Danato pushed through the entrance, and despite Ethan's silent objection to it all, he followed without delay. She, on the other hand, maintained a comfortable distance behind them.

She expected to see cells and parallel hallways similar to the other levels when she passed through the doorway, but it wasn't divided at all. It was one giant room.

The extensive floor contained a half sphere. The giant foggy snow globe was two stories high, nearly meeting the full expanse of the room's height. The width extended just short of the building's exterior walls. She couldn't see how deep it went, but she assumed that the east elevators would bring her fairly close to the opposing side of the anomaly. Within the depths of the blurry dome, she could make out images that looked like people.

Off to one side was a raised lookout, posted with two guards. Electrical equipment filled the cubicle from top to bottom. The blinking lights, buttons, dials, and doodads were demanding immediate attention. It was the first technology outside of an oven that she had seen in the prison.

"What is this?" Cori asked.

"This is the wizard's den," Ethan answered blandly as he crossed his arms and looked over the bubble like it was his long-lost enemy. "Why are we here?" He looked at Danato to answer that question. Danato gave Ethan a hard look and walked away without responding. He called one guard down from the booth and had a quiet conversation with him.

Cori sidestepped to Ethan and whispered, "Seriously, what's this all about?" She was used to Danato keeping her in the dark for her own protection, but this was the first time his lack of honesty didn't seem to favor her wellbeing.

Ethan glanced between her and Danato before answering her question. "This is a time bubble. The wizards are ultimately more powerful than any of us, so this is the only way they can be contained."

"How powerful?" Cori questioned.

"They can do virtually anything to you with their minds."

"Like what?"

Ethan rolled his eyes. "Anything, Cori: blow up your head, throw you into a rock... you're like a doll in their world."

"Why are we here?" She reached out to touch the bubble.

Ethan pulled her hand down. "I don't know. I'd like to know myself, especially if it involves going back in there."

"You've been in there before?"

Ethan's brow dipped slightly. "I've seen every level of this prison."

Her mouth gaped. "Even the top level?"

He nodded.

"And?" she asked, searching his eyes for a clue about the contents of that world.

"And what?" Ethan shrugged.

"What's up there?" she asked.

"I want Cori to go in for five hours," Danato announced behind them.

"What?" Ethan pushed past Cori and stood face to face, or at least face to chin, with Danato. "She won't last five minutes in there, let alone five hours."

Cori came into the mix, and they formed an arguing triangle of chin to face, neck to face, face to chest. "Give me some credit, Ethan! Danato, I can certainly handle myself for a few hours!"

"Cori," Ethan protested, "you don't know what you're talking about."

"Five hours," Danato repeated resolutely.

"No! She's not ready for that!" Ethan yelled, practically spitting in Danato's face.

"Yes!" Cori yelled at him before turning to Danato. She took a step back when Danato's hand flew up.

He pointed to the bubble. "*Both* of you, five hours, and that's not a concession. If you two could stop arguing for five fucking minutes, and remember who is in charge here, I would have explained that."

"Why are you doing this now? She isn't prepared. I barely survived last time."

Cori was about to object to his comment regarding her preparedness, but she didn't like the sound of "barely survived."

"Because I can't handle any more of the bickering and fighting," Danato stated.

Ethan glanced at Cori and shook his head. "This is a punishment?"

"This is a test for her, an exercise for you, and hopefully a respite for me." Danato motioned to the bubble.

"Five hours won't be much of a respite for you," Ethan said, stepping toward the bubble.

"It's more than enough time for you two to hash out this..." Danato fluttered his fingers in their faces, "...whatever this is."

Cori didn't understand why this little field trip was causing so much friction between the men, but she knew better than to stand between a bear and his cub, so she didn't bother asking any more questions.

Ethan presented his hand to Cori. She approached the bubble, but didn't take his hand. She even pulled away when he tried to hold it. She was about to reach her full fume about his assumptions about her abilities. Granted, she had no idea what was about to happen, but she didn't need to be coddled like a child. "I think I can handle it without a babysitter," she sassed.

Ethan took a deep breath and put his head down.

Danato stepped close behind her. His breathy voice against her ear made her jump. It was his calm, quiet rumble that usually signaled his true ire, not so much the loud blustering he had offered earlier. It had been a while since he had directed his anger at her. The short-lived benefit of a mourning period, she supposed.

"He's been in this bubble before," he said. "So I strongly advise to follow his lead if you want to survive. Understand?" She nodded. "Good. Now take his fucking hand so you don't end up three miles apart!" he growled before stomping away.

She threw her hand out to Ethan. She forced herself to push through the situation, rather than do what she wanted to, which was run home and cry. Ethan took her outstretched hand and gave her a little stroke with his thumb. She didn't look at him, but she knew he was offering an empathetic expression. He was not unfamiliar with Danato's wrath, and yet he always held his own against him.

Ethan drew her forward, guiding her into the bubble. As they stepped in, Cori felt her body tug into multiple directions and then fall at super speed. She would have screamed, but she couldn't figure out where her mouth was.

A s soon as they hit the water, Ethan lost Cori's hand. They rolled down the river, slamming into rocks and plummeting down miniature waterfalls. He caught a tree branch and pulled himself onto a mossy rock.

He scanned the river upstream and down for Cori. She was nowhere in sight.

He cursed and made his way to the bank by hopping rock to rock. He walked down the river, calling her name. A quarter mile down, he found her hugging her knees at the edge of the water.

He ran to her and skidded into a sitting position beside her like she was home plate. "You okay?" he asked, looking over her body for cuts and bruises, of which there were many.

Her eyes were bloodshot and her lips were blue, but she gave him a thumbs-up. After which she started coughing up more water. Ethan patted her back to help with the effort. When she finished, she smiled back at him.

He smiled and shook his head. "Why are you smiling?"

"Do you think we would still be here if I had given you the cocoa puffs?"

He laughed. She laughed, but stopped, wincing in pain.

"I think we would have ended up here eventually, anyway. He just sped it up so he could get some peace." Ethan helped her up, and she went through another bout of coughing, which he again patted her back to assist.

"How could five hours give him peace?" she asked. "Doesn't he know we'll be arguing more after five hours than when we left?"

"The time bubble doesn't follow the same timeline as the prison. Come on." Ethan ushered her upstream to change the subject. He didn't want to delve into the question-and-answer portion of their excursion yet. "We'll be safer if we can stay out of view. I know a few places we can go. No luxury hotels, though."

An hour later, they found the first of his three spots: An old shack of a cabin, built between two mountainous rocks. The wood structure was so overgrown with ivy and moss that it looked invisible to the glancing eyes.

Inside, the one-room structure held a fireplace with a cooking pot, a bed with moth-eaten sheets, a counter with base cupboards, and a single rocking chair accompanied by a banjo.

Cori looked over the room with reserved revulsion. "Certainly not the Hilton."

"It's a lot better than the other two places. Just be glad we got the river entrance."

"Yes, apart from almost drowning, I was just thinking that."

He smiled at her quip and moved to search the cupboards. "If we're lucky… and we're not." He pulled out a can of lima beans.

"I don't suppose there is a change of clothes in there?" Cori asked.

Ethan looked at her wet clothes. Her jeans were no doubt heavy with moisture and her t-shirt was bordering on being part of a bar contest. "Check beneath the mattress. There might be some pajamas."

Cori lifted the flimsy mattress and pulled out a flannel nightgown with more holes than the sheets. "I don't think this qualifies as clothing anymore." She held it up for him to see.

"Sorry. Soggy clothes it is." Ethan threw her the can of beans. "If you can open that, we'll at least have something to eat for breakfast. I'm going to get some wood to start a fire." He stopped at the entrance and tapped the doorknob. He looked back at her, debating how much authority he should exert on her. There was no official ranking between them, but he considered himself, at least in this situation, to be in charge. He didn't want to be overbearing, but she had a tendency to find trouble. He was certain it was just in her nature, but many of her entanglements could have been avoided if she had just made smarter choices. "Will you stay here?" he asked, so he didn't sound like it was an order.

Her brow crinkled. "I have nowhere to be."

His lips ticked into a smile. That would have to be good enough. He left her alone to figure out the lima beans.

Outside, he found plenty of dead wood. He picked up the driest pieces and a little brush for kindling. Upon his return to the cabin, he saw the smoke stack already going. He dropped his bundle and ran back to the cabin.

Bursting in the door, prepared to fight whatever wizard had intruded, he found Cori alone. She was crouched beside the fire, wrapped in a sheet. Ethan approached her with shoulders squared and ready to fight with her instead. "I asked you to stay here."

"Wait." She stood and held up her hands in surrender. "Watch." She stepped to the back wall of the cabin and opened a trapdoor. Inside the cubby was a stack of wood. "It even comes with its own lighter." She grabbed two flint rocks stashed with the wood and tapped a spark from them.

Ethan breathed a sigh of relief and approached her. He looked over at her outfit. "What are you wearing?" he asked indignantly, despite the smile on his face.

"A sheet. My clothes are drying on the rafters." She pointed up to the wooden beams holding her clothes, including her unmentionables. Ethan shied away from the lace white bra hanging just above his head. "Don't worry, it's not mistletoe." Cori laughed. She stopped and grabbed her side. "I bruised deeper than I thought."

"What am *I* supposed to wear?" Ethan said, leaning against the "kitchen" cupboards.

"I left the fitted sheet." She pulled the tattered bottom sheet off the bed and tossed it to him.

He observed the moth snack. "It's full of holes."

She smiled. "As long as the holes don't line up with anything special, you'll be perfectly prudish." She laughed again, then hissed in discomfort. "Damn it."

"What is wrong with you?"

"Sore, I guess."

Ethan shook his head. "Take a deep breath." She did so with no problem. "Raise your arms." She checked her knot on her sheet and raised her arms. He reached over to feel her side. She flinched, but didn't pull away from him as he searched down her side for any source of pain. His concern was a bruised rib, but there was only one thing that preceded her pain. "Laugh."

"What?" She raised an eyebrow and put down her arms.

"Go on."

She attempted to laugh, but it was forced, and didn't amount to more than a giggle. "See, nothing."

"Yeah, nothing," he said, even more curious about the pain. "Turn around," he instructed.

Cori took a baby step back. "Why?" Ethan tried not to be offended by it.

"Because I'd like some privacy." He pulled off his shirt before she had turned around. He didn't see any reason to hide what she had already seen last night. She smirked at his exhibition. He tipped his brow as if to double-dog dare her and unzipped his pants. She spun around before he made it to the end of his zipper.

"Are you sure about that?" she muttered.

After he slipped out of his clothes, he wrapped the sheet around him, careful to place the holes inconspicuously. He slipped his underwear on his head like a hat and asked Cori to turn around. She turned, and he did his best hula dance for her. She laughed heartily at his absurdity until pain arched her back.

"See, now that isn't normal." He pulled the underwear off his head and started examining her back. He poked and prodded at her spine to see if a disc had slipped or vertebrae had twisted.

"Hey, I haven't covered all the holes back there."

"Let me look behind you," he said.

"You are!" She ripped away from him and found sanctuary in a corner.

Ethan leaned against the wrought-iron frame at the base of the bed. "I need to see over your shoulder," he explained.

"Why?"

"You may not be having internal pain, well, at least not... I don't want to jump to conclusions. Can I just please look over your shoulder?"

Cori threw her head back against the wall and grunted. "I hate you, I hate you, I hate you," she grumbled as she slunk back over to him.

"Oh, relax. Bring your shoulders back." He pushed her shoulders to attention. "Good, now hold still, please." He held her shoulders in a tight grip as he leaned in over her right shoulder. He stopped just next to her ear to whisper to her. "I thought the underwear was a nice touch, don't you?"

She chuckled.

Ethan peeked over her shoulder hurriedly, just in time to get a view of a tiny rat-sized gremlin creature. The little bugger hissed and slashed at his face. "Ahh!" He pulled back, wiping his cheek where it had nicked him. "Little bastard."

"What?" Cori spun around, trying to find the source of the excitement. "What happened?"

"You have a demon parasite," he said.

"What?" She spun around, grasping at her back.

"Cori, it's not visible to you. It's a demon."

"Get it off me!" She spun around again, coming dangerously close to losing her sheet.

"Cori, it's not a spider! I can't just brush it off you."

"Why is it there?" She settled for standing by the fire and using a framed mirror from the wall to look behind her.

"It's a sorrow demon. It jumps on when someone experiences a great loss."

She stopped searching for the creature and put down her mirror. "Oh. How long does it stay?"

Ethan could see her put the pieces together in her mind. He could also tell she was agitated by the idea of anything demon or otherwise being attached to her. "As long as you are actively sorrowful or until someone... or something replaces the loss."

"I don't consider myself actively sorrowful." She stood up and adjusted her sheet. "I don't constantly mourn..."

"Last night you said that you feel guilty when you don't mourn him. That demon has been taking advantage of that. He reminds you of him, when you haven't thought of him in a while, doesn't he?"

Her face contorted with this new revelation. "I thought my mind was just stuck on a thought."

"Yeah, *his* thought. It's a very limited psychic link. He can't influence you, but he can drive you berserk if you don't make an active effort to ignore him."

"What do you mean by 'replace the loss'?"

"In this case, I think you would need to acquaint yourself with another." She shook her head, not understanding his subtext. Ethan smiled through blushed cheeks. "You need to get laid."

Cori's face muddled with a mix of emotions. After a moment, her chin raised. "Okay, let's do that."

"Huh?" Before Ethan could question her thought process, she had shoved him over the bed rail and onto the bed. "Cori..."

Cori jumped on him and kissed him fervently on the mouth. He kissed her back, allowing himself to get a taste of her before fighting against every will and desire in his body. He pushed her away. "What the hell, Cori?"

"I want this thing off me."

Ethan could see the determined panic in her eyes. Cori was not a patient person. Impetuous, impulsive, reckless. That was her all the time, but Ethan wasn't. He had no intention of letting Cori throw herself at him just to get a sorrow demon off her back. Besides, if she didn't really want to be with him, she might spiral herself deeper into the creature's clutches. "You don't need to do this. It will go away on its own. You just have to be patient."

"This will be faster."

Ethan rolled her off him before she could go in for another kiss. She landed with a thunk on the floor. He leaned over to look at her. "I may have simplified the solution by phrasing it as I did. Getting laid is not the solution, but introducing a loving relationship into your life would distract you from your sorrow and break the demon's connection to you."

Cori sat up and tucked her knees to her chin to pout over her circumstance.

"I wish it was that simple. God, how I wish it was." Ethan moved away from her before he thought about what he had just done. He knew Cori's feelings for him were changing. He could see that she looked at him differently. Unfortunately, they didn't have the option of a one-night stand or a short-term relationship. They were stuck with each other in good times and bad, whether or not they liked it.

She was in a fragile state with the loss of Vince, and anything he did to push her, or even too openly receive her, could backfire on him. The bottom line was she needed to come to him of her own free will, with no strings, or he wouldn't let himself have her. No matter how frustrated he got.

Ethan stood by the fire, warming himself. Cori must have realized how stupid she was being and followed him to the fire. "Sorry, I'm just used to looking for the easy way out."

"Just because I'm a guy doesn't make me easy," he snapped.

Cori smiled warmly. "I meant the situation. I thought I was done running away from my problems."

Ethan nodded. He raised his hand to brush a hair from her face. She didn't flinch. They locked eyes for a moment and he pulled his hand back. He could hardly move without creating an opening for intimacy.

They both looked into the fire.

"So when are you going to tell me how long *five hours* is?"

"Five days."

E THAN ROLLED OVER ON the bed and peeked at the
floor in front of the fireplace. After the sum total of
debate about the stench on the mattress versus the hard
floor, Cori opted to take the floor. In hindsight, Ethan
thought she might have gotten the better deal.

Cori wasn't by the fireplace anymore.

He sat up and scanned the room. She was gone. He
looked again, hoping his foggy morning eyes were to
blame, but the one-room cabin was a quick study. With
his pants already serving as his pajamas, he finished his
ensemble with shoes and shirt and ran outside.

He didn't have to run far before he saw Cori speaking
with an older gentleman in gauzy robes: the telltale sign of
a wizard.

C ORI HADN'T SLEPT THE best, but there wasn't much point in complaining since she had chosen the floor to begin with. She had been tempted to slip into the bed with Ethan, but given her earlier panicked behavior, she didn't want to make things any more awkward.

It had been too early to wake Ethan, but too late for her to get back to sleep. Instead, she slipped on her shoes and went outside to find something to eat.

Without going too far, she couldn't find any berries or seeds, but she found wild mint and lavender. She wasn't sure what the combination would taste like, but stranger teas had been created.

On a small bush at the edge of the path, she saw something resembling a pink rose, and she leaned down to smell it.

"I wouldn't smell that one, if I were you," said a nasal voice behind her. "Quite the nap you'll take."She cursed under her breath and looked back at the graying man with slicked-back hair and a goatee. She smiled broadly. It was the only defense she could think of, outside of just playing dead.

"Women don't exist here. Are you a spell?"

She stopped her foolish grinning and considered what she could be if she wasn't a woman. "I don't know for sure. Do you think I am a spell?" she asked.

"No, I think if you were a spell on me, you would be naked."

Cori looked down at her blue jean attire. "I am not naked, nor do I plan to be."

"If you are not a spell, you are a costume." The gray man raised his hands as if to perform an act of martial arts on her.

"A costume," Cori laughed. "How can I be a costume?"

"Who is under this vision? Mercledes? Dolf?"

Cori shook her head. "If I were those individuals, I wouldn't have tried to smell that dangerous flower."

"Maybe, but Dolf is rather stupid. If you are not a costume or a spell, then you are real."

Cori nodded. As soon as she did, the gray man's eyes changed from curiosity to cunning. He took a step at her and she stepped back.

"I haven't felt a real woman in decades."

"And you won't now." Ethan's voice came up from behind.

Cori looked back in relief. As soon as she did, he stepped between them, facing her. He grabbed her left shoulder with his left hand, while his right hand came across her face.

The impact on her face was light, but he shoved her shoulder hard, sending her flying to the ground. To the wizard, it would have appeared to be a harsh slap. She saw the gray man still studying her. She rubbed her cheek for effect.

"Who are you?" The gray man barely looked at him.

"I am the wizard Ethan."

"I am–"

"You are the wizard Demnok," Ethan interrupted him. "I know of your feats."

"I know none of yours," Demnok challenged.

"I am not so boisterous in the retelling of my tales. My work speaks for itself. Perhaps you know of the raid in Pavilion, or the quest of Wii?"

Demnok paused. "Yes, I know of these triumphs. I have heard many great things about Wii."

"My name is the only name to be associated with these feats. Do you deny my privilege to this woman? Do you challenge my experience and capability?"

Demnok paused again. He eyed Cori. "No," he said reluctantly. "I shall explore this name Ethan further." Demnok threw his stole over his shoulder. "Till we meet again." He strolled off with his nose in the air.

After he was out of earshot, Ethan looked at Cori. She had kept up the act of a traumatized child until he looked at her.

Cori waited for him to speak or yell. He just looked at her. When she couldn't take his gaze anymore, she spoke. "Oh hell, get it over with."

He looked taken aback. "Get what over with?"

"Aren't you waiting to yell at me for leaving the cabin?"

"No." Ethan shook his head. "I was waiting for you to yell at me for manhandling you."

"Was it necessary?" she asked.

"Very much," Ethan said sternly.

"Then no worries. We've done worse to each other over the last Twinkie."

"True." Ethan offered her a hand up, which she took. "Was leaving the cabin necessary?"

Cori grimaced and shoved her herbs in his face. "Tea," she followed up with a toothy grin.

He pulled her hand down and smelled the herbs. "Can't argue that." He put his hand on her back and gently rubbed along her spine. The soothing gesture felt good, which consequently made her a little uncomfortable. "I didn't hurt you, did I?"

She shook her head.

"Good." He stopped the tender contact and cuffed her on the back before heading back to the cabin.

Cori shook off the residual sensation from his touch, along with the mental taunts from her sorrow demon.

7

WITH A VERY LONG walk ahead of them, Ethan was glad to have tea in the morning, but it only staved off his hunger for a few hours. He had hoped to forage for something while walking, but everything seemed to be out of season. The thick grassy underbrush left out the option for mushrooms, and the tall lanky trees were not the fruit-bearing type.

A misty rain came in from the cliffs far to the east, leaving them cold and wet. The same misty rain that rarely left the time bubble without a dense blanket of ominous fog. It was good for keeping a low profile, but bad for traveling.

"Why are we leaving the nice, warm cabin?" Cori asked, trudging behind him.

"Demnok will come back. It's best to keep moving. Plus, we have no food." He didn't want to mention that the boredom of staying in that house another day might force him to make bad choices in the name of entertainment.

"Can't we kill a rabbit or something?" she said, dragging the leaves off a nearby branch as she passed.

"There are no rabbits here, just snakes. They're pretty easy to catch, but not so easy to kill."

"How's that?"

Ethan abruptly turned around. "Please don't ask about snakes. It's a bad experience all around, and I hope to avoid it as long as possible."

"Sorry," she said, wide-eyed with a hint of sarcasm.

Ethan grabbed her hand and pried her fingers apart, revealing the leaves she had just pulled from the branch. "And for crap's sake, stop leaving a damn beacon trail for Demnok to follow."

Cori looked at her hand. "Oh, I didn't think about that. Sorry," she said without the undertone of sarcasm.

They continued for another half mile. She was quiet as a mouse behind him. He glanced back several times to ensure that she hadn't wandered off. This was the longest amount of time he had ever spent alone with Cori, but he knew silence wasn't something that came naturally to her, especially when she had questions. He stopped and turned to her. "You can talk."

Her mouth went slack. "I wasn't *not* talking intentionally. This place seems to agitate you. I just figured the questions were making you cranky."

"Now the silence is making me cranky," he grumbled.

"*You* could talk," she pointed out before he could continue walking.

"Talk about what?" he asked, flummoxed by the suggestion.

"You could answer all my questions before I ask them, so I don't have to ask them."

"What are you questioning?"

She raised her hands to the sky. "Pick a bubble and its contents."

"Oh." He turned around and kept walking.

She stopped following and started walking beside him. "It must be in the books somewhere that once you read enough about this prison, you have to start acting reserved and enigmatic."

"I'm not trying to be secretive. I just don't know where to start."

"I'll start," Cori said, putting a skip in her step to keep up with his pace. "We are in a time bubble in which for every one hour that passes outside of it, one day passes inside of it." Cori offered Ethan the continuation with a wave of her hand.

"The bubble was actually created by a creature of sorts. We just maintain it and utilize it as containment for the wizards."

"How..." Cori stopped herself and physically zipped her mouth shut.

Ethan smiled and resisted the urge to touch her in some way. "The prison, as you know, is filled with some sentient beings, and some not so sentient. We also know that some beings are more tangible than others." Ethan nodded to her back, where she housed one such non-tangible being. "Those beings aren't necessarily prisoners here; they are just the result of magical forces being drawn into an area of highly concentrated magic.

"For those beings more sentient, and less dangerous, or more easily bound, we can negotiate living conditions and food perks in exchange for useful powers. The time bubble is actually the reason we can't have television or radio."

Ethan could see Cori bite her lip in response to that new information. He could see the questions brimming behind her eyes, but she patiently drank in his words. It was rare that she came to him for answers. Danato was usually her teacher. He liked being the teacher for once.

"The being that controls the bubble is linked to the mechanized devices that run the building. It's a non-tangible entity that feeds on electrical energy. That is its perk for keeping the time bubble going. However, televisions and radios are communication devices that would allow the being to not only transfer out of its defined parameters, but into a human being."

"That's possible?"

"It would feed off of the electrical brain impulses, all the while driving the host like a car. Escape is unheard of for this particular creature, so constant electrical feeding, and no temptation of escape, is the best way to keep it happy."

"How does—"

"Don't ask me how the time bubble works. They only offer theories, and the equations that go with it are as Greek as it gets. I just use a blanket explanation of *magic* for that one."

"What about the phone?"

"The phone is less dangerous because it doesn't produce independent broadcasts, but Danato never stays on the line for more than ten minutes at a time."

"Just when you think you have a grasp on it all, they throw time bubbles in."

"There we are." Ethan pointed across a clearing to a teepee set amidst the trees. Above the door flap were two symbols that resembled eyes. From this distance, it looked like the head of a giant, albeit a pointy one.

"Really?" Cori said, looking at the structure.

"It's warm, out of the rain, and the wizards tend to avoid this area," Ethan pointed out.

"Should we gather some wood?"

"We won't need it." He smiled and walked on.

When they reached the teepee, he undid the tied flap doors. Upon opening, the teepee expelled a waft of steam like an exhaled breath in winter. He climbed into the welcoming warmth within.

The teepee was dimly lit by the hole at the top. The floor wasn't dirt, but instead several overlapping animal hides that created a carpet. In the center was a black boulder. "What is that for?" Cori pointed to it after she slipped in behind him.

Ethan closed the flaps, adding to the dim. "It's the heater. Don't touch it; it's hotter than it looks."

Without touching it, Cori extended her hands to feel the heat from it. She pulled back when it got too warm. "Geothermal heat at its best?"

"Very good." Ethan prepared a bed for himself amongst the animal skins. He was ready to relax even if it wasn't officially night yet. After a long day of walking and breakfast as a distant memory, he didn't see any point in wasting his energy.

"How does this land get inside the prison?" Cori explored the leather walls of the teepee, which were littered with drawings. The majority of them were just bored scribbles and graffiti, but a few looked like real Native American drawings.

"Technically, we're not in the prison anymore, we are wherever this place is. We were transported here. We are bound within the limits of the bubble's designated space. The only way in and out is through the fracture in the prison."

"So, no rabbit stew?" Cori sat down beside him, as close to the stone as was comfortable.

Ethan shook his head.

Cori's stomach grumbled at the mention of stew. "We won't die of starvation in four days," she said, more to herself than him.

"Nope." Ethan leaned back on his makeshift pillow of rolled-up hide and closed his eyes.

Cori lay down, using Ethan's stomach as her pillow. He was surprised she was allowing such a close proximity, but he certainly wouldn't shove her away.

She rolled over to face him with her cheek pressed into the base of his ribs. He could feel her, but he didn't want to open his eyes to look at her. He raised an eyebrow, sensing her impending question.

"That other creature we were discussing earlier? Is it the only animal here?" she said coyly.

"It was placed inside the bubble instead of the zoology level, because it multiplies rapidly, provides food for the wizards, and it needs space to... dig."

"Couldn't we try to get one of those?" her voice chimed with childish persuasion. She even went so far as to tiptoe her fingers up his chest.

He snatched her fingers and opened his eyes. "Don't."

"Don't what?" she said, still playing her part.

"Don't play the seducer with me."

"I'm hungry, that's all." She pulled her fingers away and sat up.

"Then ask me. I don't need you blurring any lines I haven't already blurred myself."

Cori swallowed and inhaled deeply. "Can you kill a snake for us to eat?" She said it flatly, with no hint of feminine guile.

"Not unless one pops out of the dirt. You can't track them underground," he said.

"They tunnel that deep?"

"Yes."

"A snake that tunnels deep underground? What does it eat?" she asked.

"Dirt," he said.

"Dirt," she laughed. "Snakes don't eat dirt, worms eat dirt."

Ethan didn't respond. He had already said too much.

"It's a worm?" She snorted.

"It's not a worm. It's eight feet long and as thick as my thigh."

"Does it have fangs or a visible mouth?" she asked.

"No, but..."

"It's a worm!" She laughed raucously, grabbing at her side.

"Here." Ethan pulled out a granola bar he had stashed in his pocket. He'd intended to save it for day three or four, but he wanted her to shut up. He tossed the green package at her, hitting her in the head.

"Hey." She picked it up and examined it. "You had this the whole time?"

Ethan rolled over away from her. "I was saving it. I thought we might need it later."

"Only if we don't find a..." Cori ran her finger up Ethan's back. "...s-s-snake."

He rolled back to face her and pointed to the other side of the rock. "Go over there and eat your granola bar. Leave me in peace to rest."

She ignored the graveness in his voice. "Don't you want half?" She fluttered it in his face.

"No, just eat it." He waved it away.

"Well, that's a first." Cori crawled to her side of the black rock. "I guess we've come a long way, if we aren't fighting over the last piece of decent food." She stared at the package for a long moment instead of opening it. She tossed it back to him, hitting him in the stomach. He picked it up and waited for an explanation from her. "Keep it for now. I'll be way more irritable tomorrow. You'll want to give it to me then."

He wondered if they had made progress. Neither one of them was willing to claw the other's eyes out for the only processed food in the entire bubble. Or perhaps they were just too tired to make the effort. "If we come across a... worm, I'll try to kill it," he conceded.

Content with their compromise, they each lay down to rest.

E THAN JUMPED FROM HIS slumber hearing screams from Cori. Still paralyzed from his own sleep, he stumbled across the animal hides to her side. Not a soul was touching her, but her cries said otherwise.

He fell down beside her and shook her vigorously. Her arms flailed, and she arched her back. Her hastened breath hissed through tightly clenched teeth. Her eyes fluttered open, and she threw a fist at his chin.

He couldn't stop the hit, but with continued effort, he managed to restrain her arms.

"No," Cori whimpered. "Don't touch me."

"It was just a dream, Cori."

"No, it was real." She shook her head insistently. "I saw it. I felt it." She stopped flailing, but started twisting her wrists to be free of his hands. He let go, satisfied that she wouldn't punch him again.

"I know. I know." Ethan sat up beside her. "I forgot about the dreams." Ethan kicked himself for not warning her about this. Being outside of the house meant losing the luxuries of the protection the house offered.

"Nightmares," she said.

"Yes, *Freddy* would be pleased with these nightmares." Ethan rubbed the sleep from his eyes. "We aren't protected from dream feeders in this place."

"Something is eating my dreams?"

Ethan nodded and gave up trying to wake up. "Sort of. I can think of at least seven prisoners that can enter your dreams, each with their own agenda. They give you the nightmares, and in exchange, you give them your fear, or whatever emotion they want to elicit from you."

"What do I do?"

"Nothing. They're harmless, for the most part. Just acknowledge they are dreams and try to mentally remove the invading thoughts. It takes some practice, but now that they've found you, you'll have plenty of opportunity to work on it."

Cori reached over and pinched Ethan's arm.

"Ouch!" he yelped.

"Just making sure this isn't a dream."

"You're supposed to pinch yourself." Ethan pinched her back.

"Ouch! How much longer do we have?" she asked, wiping her eyes and running her fingers through her hair.

"After a short supper of air and water, we will be done with day two."

"Three more days?" She shoved his shoulder as if it were his fault. "Why do we even have to come in here?"

"Observation. Danato likes to keep track of the wizards. Plus, he seems really concerned about the conditions inside the bubble."

"How long were you here the first time?"

"Just a day. Danato showed me the basics."

"How long the second time?"

"A couple weeks," he said.

Cori's mouth dropped, awestruck. "How did you survive here for two weeks?"

Ethan shrugged. "Keep moving. Eat what you find. Kill what you can. Avoid confrontation. It's just a lot of hide and seek."

Her face saddened, and she shook her head. He couldn't pin down the emotions flickering across her face, but she seemed mortified. "You think I'm pathetic, don't you?" she asked.

"What?" he asked, shaking his head. "Where did that come from?"

"I'm going nuts after two days, and you survived here two weeks alone."

"I didn't exactly come out very sane after two weeks. This place gets to you, whether it's two days or two weeks." Ethan shivered, thinking of his last time there.

Cori curled up on the floor, facing away from him.

He reached over and rubbed her back. "I'm glad I have somebody with me this time around. Keeps the crazy from sinking in too deep."

She rolled over to face him. "Yesterday, why didn't you agree to have sex with me?" Ethan's eyes widened and he pulled his hand away from her as if it were an incendiary device for this explosive conversation. The last bit of lethargy left his body. "Because I'm not a dick," he said with a "no duh" attitude. "I saw your distress. You were reacting, not really thinking."

"But..." Cori paused. She sat up, putting more distance between them. "That is something you would be interested in?"

Ethan cleared his throat and rubbed his face, trying to compel his cheeks not to blush. He couldn't believe she could say that so casually to him. "Yes, I think that would be an accurate statement." His cheeks burned red from his admission.

"Then you should have taken the opportunity," she said coldly. Ethan tried to hold her gaze, but couldn't. "If you want something," she continued, "you should seize any opportunity to have it, even if that opportunity is a little morally compromising."

He pinched himself to check if *he* was dreaming. Was she asking him to make a pass at her? "Are you saying you want me to... What are you saying?"

"I'm saying don't let inexperience or naivety stop you from achieving any goal. Whether that be a job, a lover, or simply an object of desire; take any opportunity you can to shine."

Ethan struggled to read between the lines. He rewound their conversation to see where she'd found her tangent. "This is about you trying to become warden, isn't it?" He hugged his knees to his chest.

"Yes. I took the opportunity to steal it from you. And you should take any opportunity to take it back."

"First of all, you haven't stolen it yet. Second, I made it perfectly clear I wouldn't roll over for you when it came to the job."

"Bullshit!" She said it so harshly he almost recoiled. As it was, he tensed as if she might attack him. "You talk the talk, but would you actually grind me into the ground to get it?" He didn't fully understand her at that moment. She was angry with him for *not* being a jerk?

"So, I should be underhanded and conniving to get the position?" he said.

"Yes, you clearly know you're more qualified for it. My behavior here only proves it."

"I should steamroll you any chance I get, is that it?"

"Yes," she said solemnly.

"Even if I hurt you in the process?"

"Of course!" Even in her state of low self-esteem, Cori still managed to be a bully.

Ethan looked at the entrance. He stood up and extended his hand to her. "Come on," he growled. She raised an eyebrow at his hand, but she took it. His fingers clamped down on hers and he guided her out of the teepee.

"Is this safe?" Cori dragged behind him through the trees.

"I never see them around sunset, I don't know why." He released her hand and scaled a stack of boulders that seemed out of place. Cori stumbled behind him at her own pace.

At the top, he sat on the highest boulder and directed her to the flat rock in front of him. After she positioned herself on the ledge, he pointed at the sunset over her shoulder. "Isn't that the most beautiful sunset you've ever seen?"

Cori looked over the sky that was on perfect display for them at this height. Layers of peach, orange, and pink were highlights to the purple haze above the tree line. The sun was small and pink amid it all. "Yes, it is," she agreed.

"I don't know what it is about this place, but the sunset is always spectacular. I watched it almost every night when I was here. It helped put things in perspective."

"Why are you showing me this?" she asked.

He lowered his forehead onto her shoulder with an exhale. "Because you need perspective," he said, leaning back. "You may still be figuring out who you are, or who you want to be, but I'm not. I've never had anybody to help define me. After my parents died, I jumped from foster home to foster home. I learned to find a home in myself.

"So believe me when I say I'm not a dick. I actually give a crap about you and your wellbeing." He leaned forward to whisper into her ear. "Maybe steamrolling is your way of getting things you want, but it's not mine. I have no intention of sacrificing my principles just so you can feel better about your tactics. You want to be the warden? Then be stronger than that cocky image you portray."

She said nothing in response. He watched the sunset, pretending that the madness of the day was melting into the ground, just like the sun.

9

T HE MORNING OF DAY three was cold and damp, but at least the rain had stopped. Ethan went out to scout the area before they could leave. Cori stayed in the tent, trying to erase the images of last night's dreams from her psyche. Having a sorrow demon reminding her about Vince's death and nightmares reliving her capture into slave labor was taking its toll on her sanity.

She heard a shout from outside the tent. She peeked out of the flap and saw Ethan with a wizard. "Damn it."

"I am the wizard Dolf," the chubby bald man announced. "Who are you?"

"I am the wizard E..." Before Ethan could answer, he was up in the air choking, while Dolf played the part of Darth Vader.

Cori wanted to run out and fight him, but given his powers, she knew it would be useless. She remembered what the first wizard had said about Dolf being dumb, and she hoped it was true.

E THAN FELT THE INVISIBLE grip tighten around his neck, and he wondered if Dolf would bore of him eventually and release him, or just kill him for sport. Without a voice, he could not even plead for mercy or surrender.

There was a low growl behind him, similar to a bear. It caught Dolf's attention as well. Unfortunately, his grip didn't waver.

The low growl stopped, and a laugh followed. Dolf's attention on him waned, and he lowered Ethan to the ground. He could breathe a little better, but his movement was limited.

He turned his head just enough to see the tent flap moving open and shut with each "ha" of the laugh, steam rising from the tent as it did.

"Why do you attack my lunch?" The deep voice spoke from within as the tent flap mouthed the words.

Ethan cringed, thinking how ridiculous this ploy was, but Dolf's eyes were big. He was buying every bit of it.

"Kill my lunch, and I will need a replacement," the tent said. "You look mighty tasty."

Without another word, Dolf released Ethan and ran off in the opposite direction. Ethan dropped to the ground and gasped. When it was clear, Cori ran out to his aid.

"I can't believe that worked," she said, raising Ethan's arms in the air so his lungs could fully expand.

"Neither can I. He must be the stupidest wizard ever."

"According to Demnok he probably is," she said.

"Demnok?"

"It was mentioned in passing when he thought I was a wizard in disguise."

"Good memory," Ethan said.

"Thanks." Cori slapped her hands together, apparently exhilarated by saving his life. "Where to today?"

He wondered how long that enthusiasm would last when they started walking again. "The caves are probably the least hospitable lodging, but the safest."

"Safe is good." Cori helped Ethan up. He wasn't really in that bad of shape, but he liked it when she took care of him. It had been a long time since he had anyone to nurture him. "I didn't know the wizards could pull a Darth Vader."

Ethan smiled. "Their powers are limited to manipulating the human body."

"Just people, not animals?"

"No." Ethan shook his head.

"Why not?"

"I don't know; something about the type of magic in them. Animals fall under a different category."

"Why are they so stupid?"

"They aren't stupid. They are insane. Granted, their insanity makes them easier to dupe, but you can't underestimate their powers. Every one of them could snap our necks with a flick of their wrists. Literally."

"Why don't they?"

"They barely remember themselves, let alone who their colleagues are. That's why I introduced myself as a wizard to Demnok. He has no idea if I'm lying, and he can hardly risk getting into a battle with another wizard. It gets bloody."

"So you just bullshit your way out of trouble?"

"Yep." Ethan nodded. "As long as I am a mystery, I am safe."

"Why did Dolf attack you then?"

"He must have seen me scouting the area. He must have known I wasn't one of them."

"Close call, huh?"

Ethan smiled. "Not with the great and powerful teepee at my back."

Cori nodded, but didn't smile at his quip.

10

ETHAN WAS HAPPY TO have someone to keep him company on his travels this time around. He wasn't, however, entirely prepared to entertain that someone. Cori hadn't taken well to the long walking and her hunger had changed from cranky to something far worse: feisty. "You know what I hate the most about this place," Cori said loudly as she traipsed along behind him. "The walking. Walk here. Walk there. I am so sick of walking."

Ethan pulled the granola bar from his bag and tossed it over his shoulder to her. She caught it. "This won't change how I feel about walking," she said, brandishing the bar at him when he glanced back.

He didn't stop or respond to her. He felt a push from behind. He stumbled forward a few steps and turned around. "What do you want me to do about it, Cori?"

"I don't know," she said, frustrated.

"Do you want to stop and rest?" He felt as if he was talking to a two-year-old that needed a nap, but refused to fall asleep.

"No," she moaned. "How much further?"

"Longer than you want it to be," he said. "Eat the granola bar. You'll feel better."

"I don't want to eat the granola bar. *You* don't need a granola bar."

"Cori!" He turned around to face her. "Either eat it, or rest, or shut the hell up. I don't want to get attacked again because you want to starve competitively."

She abruptly sat down Indian style with a huff and started eating the granola bar. "I hate this place," she mumbled with her mouth full. Half way through, she offered the rest to Ethan. He nodded for her to finish it. "Please eat it, so I don't have to feel like an ass." She thrust it up at him.

He sat down beside her and finished the last bit of granola. He didn't want to admit that it was the best-tasting granola bar he had ever eaten. After he finished, he started to get up. Cori pushed him again, making him land on his butt. He stared at her, flabbergasted. "What the hell?"

"I am willing to do anything to avoid walking again, including pick a fight with you."

"I'm not fighting you," he said firmly.

"Okay," she said.

He started to get up again, but she hooked his ankles with her feet and pulled him down again. He glared at her, but she just laughed.

"Cori! This is childish."

"I know, I know, but this walking is so boring. I think I have ADHD." She crawled toward him.

He jumped to his feet before she could stop him. "No, you're just spoiled."

She kneeled before him, grabbing his shirt. "Wait, wait, wait, I have an idea."

He pulled away and started walking.

"It involves taking our clothes off."

He couldn't help but be intrigued. He stopped and looked back at her. She smiled mischievously and tipped her brow.

CORI RAN THROUGH THE trees ahead of him, giggling like a schoolgirl. Ethan struggled to keep up, ducking the evergreen branches she left swinging in her wake. It was late afternoon, and he expected another hour's worth of walking before they reached the caves, leaving them just enough time for whatever Cori had planned.

"Come on," she called back to him.

"Where are you going?" He didn't really know why he had followed her so unquestioningly. Actually, he did.

"Come on." She giggled.

He popped out of the trees just as Cori started removing her clothes, starting with her shoes. She smiled at him, hopping on one foot to get her shoe off. Behind her in the clearing was a serene lake. The water mirrored the blue sky and late-day sun.

"You want to swim?" he asked, reasonably disappointed.

"No," she said, moving to him. "I want *us* to swim." She grabbed his hand and pulled him closer to the water. "Take your shirt off."

"How did you know this was here?" he asked, slipping his t-shirt over his head.

"I saw it last night while we were watching the sunset. I made a mental note of the surrounding landscape." She continued to remove her own shirt and pants, leaving only her underclothes.

He turned away, making an excuse to survey the area, so he wasn't tempted to openly gawk at her. "We are putting ourselves in a vulnerable position. This is foolish and dangerous." Even as he said it, he pulled off his shoes.

"Dangerous, and we get to take our clothes off. I can't believe I have to talk you into this."

He looked back at her, shifting his eyes in every imaginable direction before he could focus on her face. "Maybe I should stay out here and keep a lookout."

"You can watch out for me, in the water," she said, backing off the shore into the shallow water. She kicked the water at him. "Come on, where's that blind dedication that earned you a scar yesterday?"

Ethan grumbled a cuss under his breath and slipped out of his cargo pants. "Okay, but we have to be quiet," he said right before he yelled and charged in after her. She squealed and dove in. After a bit of splashing, they settled into the cool water and floated around.

Ethan had forgotten how freeing swimming was. It was like being a kid again.

THE REMAINING WALK TO the cave Cori didn't lag behind, nor did she complain about the walking. She kept a strange little smile on her face that Ethan couldn't help but be amused by.

He chuckled to himself after one particular glance.

"What are you laughing at?" she asked.

"You," he said. "Who knew swimming would put you in a sane state of mind?"

"Well, what do you expect? We live in Siberia. We don't have a pool, at least not one that isn't filled with sea creatures. When else are we going to swim?"

"That's true. I never thought of that," he said.

"See, you should thank me for providing you with a long-overdue pleasure."

"Thank you." Ethan took her hand and brought it to his lips for a chaste kiss. It was a gesture he had seen Danato do many times with her. He couldn't think of a better way to express his thanks for such a liberating afternoon.

Unfortunately, his gracious gesture was spoiled when she yanked her hand back. She must have seen the shock in his face, because she looked away. He wasn't sure what was more offensive to him: that she pulled away from him, or that she looked away.

He couldn't understand her. One minute they were friends, skirting the options of being more, and the next they were complete strangers to each other. This was why he couldn't seek her out. This was why no matter what he felt for her, he wouldn't push a relationship with her until she asked for it.

He walked on ahead of her, no longer wanting to observe her smile. He heard her mumble, "you're welcome" from behind as he distanced her.

When they finally reached the cave, Ethan started a fire and lay straight down to sleep. Cori sat across the fire, poking at the wood with a stick. Sparks glittered out from the wood as she did.

"Are you awake?" she finally asked.

"That depends on what you want." He had sensed a shift in her demeanor. She was unsettled. He wasn't sure if it was in regard to the awkward hand kiss or just frustration over the lack of entertainment. Either way, he wasn't committed to playing the role of the concerned friend.

"Nothing, I guess," she said.

"You definitely have ADHD," he grumbled and rolled over, putting his back to her.

"I just..." Cori trailed off. A few seconds later, he heard a stuttered inhalation.

He looked back and saw tears in her eyes. He sat up. "What is it?"

She shook her head vigorously, trying to get herself under control before speaking. "I don't want to fall asleep," she blubbered.

"Oh, crap." Ethan chastised himself for being so blind. He crawled over to her and held her in his arms. She tensed at his touch, but he didn't release. "I'm so sorry. I forgot about the dreams. They are wicked." He rocked her slightly, while she gulped in breaths. "That bad, huh?" he whispered in her ear.

"Yes." She nodded. "It's just my memories, but with more violence, and in vivid Technicolor. Those stupid assholes! I hate them so much for doing this to me."

"You can stop the dreams. If you..."

"What?" She sniffled.

"It took me a few nights to get the hang of controlling them. It just takes mental preparation and a safe place in your mind."

"Nothing I could learn in under an hour." Cori laughed through her tears.

"No." Ethan grimaced.

"I hate this. I thought I was over this. The fear." She pulled away from him. He released her, feeling the sting of rejection again. She turned to face him. "I didn't mean to pull away like that this afternoon. The dreams have put me on the defensive." She leaned down and shook her head. "The stupid sorrow demon is latching onto them, too. I feel like I'm being pulled in two different directions."

"What's the other direction?"

She looked back up at him, and he wasn't sure what she saw in his face, but she stopped crying and the sadness in her eyes was replaced with fear. "What?"

"You said two different directions."

Her mouth gaped as she stared at him. "Will you sleep with me tonight?"

It was Ethan's turn to play the slack-jawed idiot. He knew she was just trying to get out from under her fear demon, but if she was reliving the traumas of her captivity, it was even more important that he not indulge her vacillating attentions. He frowned and gave her arm a gentle rub. "Cori, we talked about that."

"Beside me," she clarified.

"Oh." He cleared his throat and let his disappointment, relief, and embarrassment out with a cathartic chuckle. "You should have said that last part a little quicker."

She ignored his quip and continued to plead with her eyes. "You can wake me up when I start to have the nightmares?"

"I'll be ready to slap you awake at a moment's notice." He smiled.

Her eyes flickered over him, just as his had flickered over her a moment earlier. She seemed to pose a question or statement that sat on the edge of her lips, waiting to be spoken. She opened her mouth, taking in the breath she needed for her words, but she stopped. Her eyes hardened, and she gave him a forced smile.

She lay down next to the fire. He scooted up next to her, trying to find the balance between protection and propriety. She fell asleep faster than he expected. Each time she started screaming, he woke her, subdued her, and lulled her back to sleep.

At some point in the night, he stirred to her heavy breathing. She was grunting and groaning and her face showed pain. Instead of waking her up, he caressed her face. "Cori, it's me. You're safe," he whispered. Her face relaxed slightly. "No one can hurt you. I'm watching over you. I'll protect you." His face was so close to hers. Her eyelids quivered, triggered by her dreams. The soft curve of her cheek glowed against the dying fire. Her lips were a rosy pink that hardly needed lipstick. He wanted to kiss her.

"I love you, Cori," he whispered into her ear. The nightmare passed. Her chest rose and fell with slow, shallow breaths. Her face no longer cringed and her muffled nightmare screams ceased.

He was so close to her now. He couldn't leave her, not yet. He lowered his face to hers. He was terrified she would wake and accuse him of molesting her.

Ever so slightly, he touched his lips to hers. Her lips were soft and warm. Without the return from her, it was hardly more than a peck, but Ethan felt better somehow. He could at least say he hadn't passed up the opportunity.

12

ETHAN WOKE UP LATE the next morning. The spot where Cori had slept was empty and already cold. "Damn it." He forced himself up and went outside to look for her. As he stepped out of the cave, he caught sight of a wizard within earshot. He ducked back in and peeked out at him.

The wizard was leaning against a tree, shining his gold medallion necklace with his long dark beard. The chain held five thick gold coins with obscure markings. His long gauzy robe was covered in blood. Ethan got the impression his necklace was newly acquired.

Ethan searched for a weapon. The rocks were all either too big or too small, and the sticks were kindling at best. He peeked back out of the cave entrance. The wizard had settled against a tree for a standing nap. His head was back and his eyes closed. Whatever he had just done to get his necklace must have taken a good deal of his energy.

Ethan cursed silently.

A pink flower fell from above the entrance to the cave. He looked at the bloom and picked it up. He looked up. Cori leaned over the cliff's edge above.

She motioned to the flower he had pinched between his fingers. She cupped her hand and put it over her nose and mouth. She took a deep breath in and pretended to fall asleep. She then pointed at the wizard.

He examined the flower. There didn't appear to be any particulate on it. *Are you sure?* He mouthed to her.

Yes, she mouthed back.

He shook his head and sneaked out of the cave. He didn't have far to go. He debated whether to accost the wizard or simply push the flower up to his face. He slipped into position behind the tree and simply reached the flower over, dangling it over the man's nose.

The man was already snoring. Ethan wasn't sure if he would know the difference if he did pass out.

After a few snores, the wizard slumped and fell over. Ethan relaxed.

Cori raced over. "Holy crap, it worked!"

"You said you were sure!" His voice pitched high.

"I was mostly sure."

"How did you know in the first place?" he asked.

"The Demnok wizard said not to smell the flower, or else I would sleep a long time." She stood over the wizard. "Now what? Do we leave?"

"No, I think we can drag him into the woods, far enough away that he'll be a little lost. He will have to assume another wizard did it to him."

Ethan picked up the wizard's torso while Cori helped with his feet. They took him several hundred yards north, away from their camp. Ethan would have preferred to take him farther, but he didn't know how long he would be unconscious.

They dropped him and Cori headed back right away. Ethan hung back. He looked at the gold medallion necklace and decided that if a wizard had attacked, they would likely have taken the jewelry.

He ripped the necklace off of him and shoved it in his pocket. It kind of felt as if he was pilfering, but it's not like Danato would let him keep it, anyway.

B ACK AT THE CAVE, Cori tried to find the last
vestiges of coals in the fire. Ethan kept an eye out
at the entrance. After a half hour with no excitement,
he brought his attention to her.

Cori noticed him watching her. At first she ignored
it, but when his contemplative stare looked more and
more like introspective torture, she joined him at the
entrance on the opposite side.

"Was there something you wanted to say to me?"
she said, putting her hands behind her back.

He averted his gaze, suddenly finding interest in
his feet. "I owe you an apology." She arched a brow
in response to the admission. "Before you left... with
Vince. I knew what a relationship with him meant. I
knew he would die young. I knew you were falling in
love with a man with a death sentence."

He's dead.

She shifted against her rock wall, not nearly as uncomfortable with the subject matter as the incessant brain hijacking. "Why tell me this now?"

"I went to see Mezula after you left. She told me that if you knew he was going to die, that you wouldn't have let yourself love him fully."

She nodded, remembering a conversation with Vince that had led her to that same conclusion. "What else did she say?"

"She said that when you returned, the only thing that would stand in the way of you loving another would be your grief."

Cori nodded, but said nothing.

"Still." He finally looked at her. "I'm sorry I didn't warn you when I had the chance."

"That's been eating at you, hasn't it?" she asked.

He nodded. "A little."

"You know, nobody told me. Danato didn't tell me. Vince certainly didn't tell me. I could have looked it up, but I didn't. I think Mezula had it right. Without that relationship, I might have been bitter forever. I needed it. I needed him." She glanced at Ethan to see if the topic was making him uncomfortable. To her surprise, he was listening and waiting for more. "I—"

A rumble disrupted her monologue. The ground outside the cave cracked.

She looked between Ethan and the broken ground. He stared out of the crack with the blank face of boredom. "Crap," he said flatly.

The ground exploded as a huge... worm catapulted to the surface. Its segmented body was ten inches thick and twelve feet long. It wriggled along the surface like an alligator with no left feet.

"Is that the worm?" Cori's mouth salivated, staring at her potential steak dinner.

"Yes."

She looked back and forth between Ethan and the worm. Her eagerness waned as she remembered how resolute he was about not wanting to hunt one. "I guess it is a bit big," she said with a grimace. "I understand if you don't want to mess with it."

Ethan growled under his breath. "I said I would."

"I can help." Her voice was cheery.

Ethan shook his head. "It really won't do any good," he said solemnly, preparing for his abuse.

"I'm pretty adaptive. I've proven that," she said defensively.

He shook his head again. "There is no strategy. There is no great challenge of wits, it's just me and him... and a rock."

Ethan's head sunk and he sulked, descending from the cave. He acted as if he had just chosen the short straw to go shoot a beloved pet. He picked through several rocks until he found one he liked. He approached the worm without stealth or cunning. He straddled the creature at the head—the end that didn't poop—and started bashing the rock into it.

Cori watched as the creature thrashed and bucked. Ethan hung on to the worm like a cowboy to a wild horse. He hit the worm repeatedly with the rock. The worm seemed unaffected by the assault.

She deliberated whether to join him in the battle, but aside from the thrashing and bucking, the creature posed no threat to him. Its only defense was a hard head. If Ethan could stay on, it was only a matter of time and energy.

Forty-five minutes later, Cori had sat down at the entrance to the cave, tossing rocks out over the edge. The worm had finally stopped moving. Ethan stumbled up the incline to the cave panting and sweaty. He collapsed next to Cori and rolled onto his back. "The only decent meat is the organ meat." He gulped for breath. "You can break the skin with a sharpened stick and tear it open. The heart is best, the liver is eatable, but I wouldn't say it's good."

"Are you okay? You look like you're having a heart attack."

"Oh, yeah, I'm great. That took me way longer last time. I'm on top of the world. I'm going to get some firewood." She thought he was being sarcastic, but he stood up and jogged off.

Cori searched for dissection tools.

ETHAN COLLECTED WOOD WITH new pride. He was pleased that his strength had increased, as well as his stamina. He aspired to kill a worm with three strikes, just as Danato had claimed to. Although he wondered if that had been an exaggeration.

Drowning in self-satisfaction, he didn't notice the wizard watching him from the trees until it was too late.

A branch snapped ahead of him. He looked up and saw a gaunt old wizard sneering at him from within the tree line. He was frail, but he knew that only meant he was strong enough to survive to an advanced geriatric age. Panic set in and he contemplated his options: confront the old man with attitude, bow abjectly and beg for his life, or simply walk away and hope he had no interest in following him.

Before he could decide, Cori emerged from the brush to his left, covered in blood from her face to her waist. She carried the fresh, bloody worm's heart. The horrific choking sound she made was so real he almost thought for a second something had actually happened to her. She stumbled into the clearing mimicking a zombie and collapsed to her knees.

He glanced at the wizard in the trees and saw his eyes widen with shock.

He crossed his arms and put on his best maniacal smile.

Cori held out the heart for a sacrificial offering before she collapsed face first before him. He placed his foot gently on her back and laughed loudly, like a supervillain or mad scientist.

The wizard scurried away deep into the trees. Ethan reduced his laugh to a legitimate chuckle and removed his foot from her back. She rolled over and raised the heart. "All I have to offer you," she said in a southern drawl, "is my heart."

Ethan smiled at her not because of her jest, but because she had just averted another attack and she didn't even know it. "That was quick," he said. "Did you get the liver too?"

"I can't tell what's what in there. Besides, I was a little put off when the heart exploded on me."

"Oh, I didn't mention that?" He tucked his firewood under one arm and helped her up. "Thought I had." He smiled smugly.

"You knew that would happen?" she said, dusting herself off with one hand, which only resulted in smearing more blood on her shirt.

"I killed it. You can process it," he argued. "I had to do it all myself last time. Considering it took twice as long; you can imagine how much fun I had."

"As long as I get to eat it, I don't care what explodes on me." She grimaced. "Well, that's not really true." She shivered.

Ethan laughed, but he didn't ask what she was thinking about to cause that reaction. He brought his attention back to the forest. He surveyed the perimeter to make sure no one else was around. His sudden austerity put Cori on guard. To his surprise, she sidled up next to him as if waiting for him to give the order to duck or run.

"What is it?" she said, scanning the tree line with him.

"Nothing, just checking. Thanks to your amazing skill and dumb luck, we are once again safe from all threats." He headed back toward the cave.

"What is that supposed to mean?" she asked, running up and blocking his way.

He stopped and cocked his head. "I'm sorry, that was a positive negative, wasn't it? I guess I should just stop at 'you are amazing.'" He winked and tried to move by her, but she stood firmly in his way and glared at him. He drew back, genuinely shocked by her annoyance. "Cori, I'm not trying to tease. I meant that as a compliment."

Her face went somber and her eyes searched for the meaning of the word "compliment."

"What is going on in that little brain of yours? What did I say to piss you off?"

She sighed. "It is just luck. Danato said that too. I'm one big walking accident."

"That's not what I meant."

"I know." She rolled her head back to crack her neck. She looked down at the heart. "I must be starving, because this thing looks like roast beef."

She walked on, leaving Ethan to question what it was he'd said that caused such a downshift in her jubilation.

14

WHEN HE GOT BACK to the cave, Cori was already wrapping the meat in fronds to get it ready to place on the fire. He dropped his kindling and put together a chimney-style stack in the fire pit before using flint to spark it to life. All the while, he watched Cori. He couldn't place her emotions. She wasn't happy, but she wasn't sad. She just seemed weary.

Once the fire had developed some good coals, she placed the wrapped meat in the center, pushing it into the ash. She looked like she was about to say something to him, but stopped when she saw his eyes were already on her. Confusion and shame flickered across her face before she looked away.

Normally he wouldn't have pursued the meaning of those emotions, but he wasn't satisfied with the way their previous conversation had been interrupted, and he knew she had something on her mind.

He stood up and waited for her to look at him again. When she did, he nodded to the entrance. "Come on, that thing will take forever to cook." He stepped outside and leaned against the cliff wall. The sun was setting, leaving the sky with all manner of colors to enjoy. He breathed in the watercolor serenity.

Cori propped herself on the opposite side of the entrance. She kicked her foot back to rest on a grassy outcrop. She pushed a stray hair out of her face, but discovered it was actually a piece of grass from the outcrop above her. She broke the grass off so it wouldn't interfere with her peaceful observation.

He watched her settle in to enjoy the view, but soon her eyes drifted down until she was staring at the ground rather than the sunset.

He wanted to broach the subject of her mood, but he wasn't sure how to say, "*What the hell is wrong with you?*" nicely. Again, he went back over the conversation earlier to see what he had said or done to offend her. He couldn't find anything.

She looked over at him and saw him watching her. He didn't look away. She locked eyes on him until her melancholy dragged her gaze back down to the ground again.

A riotous debate took place in his mind as he argued his options: say something, say nothing, go to her, don't go to her, or fall on your knees and profess your unwavering love and desire for her. The last one wasn't so much on the table as an option, but for some reason, his brain kept throwing it out there just in case it became viable.

"I owe you an apology, too," she said. Ethan silently rejoiced to hear her break the silence. "Maybe a few."

"For what?" he asked.

She took in a deep breath as if she was about to sink under water. "Firstly, for being me."

He wrinkled his brow and gave her a half-cocked smile. "How's that?"

"I've been selfish. I think its second nature to me. My world was in upheaval and then it was completely out of my control, and even after I was no longer in danger, I just kept fighting. As if escaping Danato would magically bring back my mother and put my life on track again. I'm sure you were going through the same thing, but I didn't even acknowledge it." She frowned at him. "I shouldn't have left you there alone."

He looked away, taking the apology as well as a gut punch. He hadn't expected an apology for that, let alone such a strict one. He shook his head to dismiss her gesture, but she continued.

"I should have placed more importance on our friendship. We came into this mess together. The least I could have done is give you a proper goodbye."

He looked back at her, still seeing the resolute determination in her confession. He couldn't keep her gaze. Her honesty was melting a deep cold bitterness he had never let go.

"I need you to know something, though. I loved Vince."

He cleared his throat of any emotional lumps that might crack his voice. "Why would you think I needed that clarified?"

"Because you had me pegged right. The day I left, you accused me of not loving him."

He groaned and threw his head back against the wall behind him. That was a memory he wished he could lobotomize from his brain. "I was so bitter; I can't tell you how much I've regretted that argument."

"I know. I understand. My point is, you were right. I was basically whoring myself out to escape."

"You are not a whore!" He spat the word out, rejecting the assessment with his fervor alone.

"No, but..." Cori's voice softened, soothing his anger. "I needed something from Vince. Something I knew I could get if I persuaded him. Vince saw right through my plan. He denied himself to me for weeks." She smiled and stared at the sunset, dazed by the fondness of the memory. She jolted and shook her head. "Shut up," she whispered to no one in particular.

"Sorrow demon?" he asked, when she came back to reality.

She nodded. "He doesn't like my good memories."

"The good memories will always win. I promise."

She gave him a subdued smile before continuing to tell her story. "I stayed because I was starting to fall in love with him and because I was terrified of the world. Somewhere between being kidnapped and..." She left the sentence incomplete. "Vince became my rock. He made the world safe again. With him I wouldn't be attacked, and if I was, let's face it, there's no competition when your boyfriend is a werewolf.

"When I got back, I was overcome with grief." She scoffed and tapped her shoulders. "Obviously. I didn't know what to do. I settled in again." She tipped her brow. "I pretended the last nine months hadn't happened, much to the dismay of my co-workers." She smiled at him. "That's my second apology. I shouldn't have assumed that those months on your own weren't difficult."

Ethan felt another kick in the stomach. This time the ache subsided quicker, but, as he had expected, the more his resentment melted, the harder it was to keep the option of professing his love for her off the table.

"Danato came to me a few weeks after I was back and offered me my freedom. It was why I left nine months earlier, but I didn't want it. I told him I wanted to stay, that I had no one on the outside. That isn't untrue, but it was really my fear that was keeping me here. I didn't have anyone to protect me out there. At least here I have Danato and you." His eyes found his way to hers again, and she grinned.

"You." She gave his full body a not-so-cursory glance. "You just had to turn into a superhero overnight. You're a born leader, commanding, but respectful. You were my next rock, just waiting to be leaned on." Her smile widened, reaching her eyes. He smiled back at her, even though he loathed hearing how this confession was going to end. "As soon as I could reconcile my grief and my guilt, I would have had you to depend on."

She shook her head and lost her smile. "I saw what I was doing, and I didn't like it. I was about to use you as a crutch, just like Vince. I wanted to stand on my own. I wanted to be my own rock. That spawned my ridiculous assumption that I might have a chance at becoming the warden. Which brings me to my third apology: I'm sorry I tried to take your job from you. Instead of leaning on you, I ended up trying to push you out of my way. I hadn't really planned on you pushing back."

He smirked, remembering the conversation that had started the bulk of their competition.

"I also hadn't planned on it being a wholly unbearable endeavor." She paused a moment before stepping away from the wall and turning to him. "When we get back, I'll inform Danato that I no longer want to compete for the position." Cori went into the cave, not offering any further discussion on the announcement.

Ethan had pondered her apologies. He was relieved to hear her acknowledge his pain, but he wasn't happy to hear she wanted to quit. He followed her in and watched her turn the heart with sticks to start it browning on the other side. "Why?" he asked.

"I just told you."

"You told me why you want the job. To prove to yourself, you can take care of yourself."

"Yeah." She put down her sticks and stood upright, wiping her hands on her jeans. "And I'm failing at it. You're stronger than I am; you're faster than I am; you're smarter than I am. I can't understand anything in those damn books. I'll never pass the final challenge. I'll be lucky to score high enough on the written to get a guard job."

"You are clever as hell!" he scolded her with his accolade. "I told Danato you wouldn't last five minutes in here, and three times now you've saved my butt. Don't sell yourself short just because you can't bench press as much as me."

"It's dumb luck, Ethan. You said it, Danato said it. Everything that I've brought to the table is just another one of my mistakes turned into a serendipitous benefit. You are the only one doing anything of value here."

"Then why does it keep happening? Maybe it isn't luck, maybe it's just you. Maybe you are that fucking amazing!" His heart was about to jump out of his chest. He couldn't believe he was arguing in defense of her, and she was arguing in defense of him. This was a very interesting turn of events.

She smiled, apparently seeing the same twist. "You are supposed to be taking advantage of this opportunity to get me off your back."

He shook his head and crossed his arms. "I don't want you off my back. I love the competition. Don't get me wrong, I'm not going to let you beat me, but that doesn't mean you can't walk away from this rivalry with your head held high. So, no, you aren't quitting, end of discussion."

"Oh, yeah?" She crossed her arms to mimic him, but the crook of her smile gave away her amusement.

"Yeah, and no more Cori-bashing, I won't have you talking like that about my friend."

She mock saluted him and crouched down to poke at the heart. He pushed away the urge to hug her. It was comforting to finally know what thoughts were clanking around in her head the last few months. However, understanding her better would only make it more difficult to deny his feelings for her. He didn't want to push her, especially since she had explained very clearly why she didn't want to be with him. But at the same time, she had also confirmed what he suspected: She was attracted to him and had considered being with him.

"You know, Cori..." She looked up from the fire. "It is possible to be a rock for yourself, and still lean on someone else when you need to." She seemed to contemplate this for a moment before nodding. She smiled warmly at him and went back to poking her meat.

15

Although the heart was chewy and far from tasty, Cori devoured almost half of it, and Ethan finished the rest. If Danato had accomplished anything by sticking them in the time bubble, he had guaranteed her complete and utter devotion to processed foods.

After a few baritone belches, Ethan announced his fatigue and lay down to sleep. When she didn't follow, he looked up at her with concern. "Aren't you tired?"

She sat watching the flames dance. A few thoughts were rambling through her mind. Once in a while, the sorrow demon would throw out his reminder, but she ignored it. "In a bit," she said with a hint of a smile.

He continued to watch her. "Are you worried about the dreams?"

She shrugged. "No, I'll sleep close." The worry etched on his face diminished, and he lay back and closed his eyes.

Cori basked in the serenity left by her cathartic day. She hadn't been that honest with anyone, including herself, in a long while. It felt good.

She looked through the fire at Ethan. He was right. She had spent so much time trying to avoid leaning on him, but it never occurred to her it wouldn't make her weak. But then, it really wasn't about rocks anymore. All the emotional cards had been dealt, tallied, and shown. No more *Go Fish* for either of them. The only thing left to ante was the attraction.

He had wanted her from day one. She had never considered him then, but now it was different. He was different. She was different. The things that mattered before either didn't matter anymore, or weren't a factor anymore.

She had been keeping her distance, trying not to be a tease. She wondered if she had kept him distant for another reason. Maybe she was afraid she would make a move on him.

Why not?

Grief? Guilt?

In the end, it was just the two of them. Vince was gone. Whether she waited another month or two to satisfy some preconceived mourning period, she was still going to want Ethan. And he was still going to want her.

She watched his chest rise and fall with his steady breath. If he knew what she was thinking right then, he wouldn't be breathing so slowly. As it was, she could feel her own heart thump harder in her chest.

He's dead.

Sorrow demon be damned. Guilt be damned. Grief be damned.

Cori crawled around the fire. For a moment, she thought he might refuse her again. She pushed the thought away and slunk up beside him. She wet her lips and made a mental plan to straddle him just as she kissed him.

She didn't want there to be any confusion about what she wanted from him. She didn't want him to think about the consequences. All she wanted was to offer him the experience he had waited so long for.

Her hands shook as she braced them on either side of his shoulders. She had never expected being with Ethan. The thrill of acting on complete impulse, with only one step planned in advance, was intoxicating.

She brought her leg across his hips but didn't touch. She got into position and prepared her simultaneous descent onto his lips, chest, and pelvis. Her heart was about to break through her chest. She leaned in, knowing that she didn't have to plan any more of the night, because she knew he would have plenty of ideas about where they should go after the kiss.

She lowered herself onto him. The movement seemed to go in slow motion. The world around her blurred. Their lips froze an inch from touching. The inch may as well have been a mile, because she couldn't move.

She screamed in frustration as she realized what was happening. She felt the distance between them stretch as the hazy world seeped in between them. She felt the hand on her shoulder, and she tried to fight against it. She wanted one more second. One more inch.

Her guttural scream caught up to her as she fell away from the time bubble into the real world. She stumbled and landed on her butt. She stopped screaming, but she could feel her teeth still clenched in a feral sneer.

Danato stepped into her field of vision and asked her something. His muffled voice was unintelligible. "What?" she said, or at least that's what she thought she said. Her voice was just as muted.

Danato pointed to the far wall under the lookout station. She saw Belus waving at her to come over. Two chairs stood next to a table behind him. A large wooden box sat on the table.

Thick, muscular arms looped into hers, and she was lifted to her feet. She confirmed her suspicions that it was Danato who had lifted her like a rag doll. He pulled her chin to face Belus again and pointed to him. The one-syllable, muffled grunt she heard from him made her feel like a child being sent to a naughty chair.

She walked over, surprised by how spry her legs were. Everything felt fine, even good, except her ears. Someone had misplaced an entire stuffed animal in each of her ears.

She sat down next to Belus, who had already taken the other seat. She pointed to her ears.

He nodded at her and pointed to his open box. It contained two rows of gold tuning forks, each stamped at the base with a number that meant nothing to Cori.

"Where's Ethan?" She probably sounded like a megaphone to Belus, but to her, it still sounded like she was talking under water.

Belus smiled, finding some amusement at her expense. He skipped the verbal communication and just pointed. She followed his finger.

Ethan had not gone far. He and Danato were only about ten meters away from her. They were facing her, but not looking at her. Instead, their eyes were fixed on a tall, leggy blonde in a red business suit she could only see the back of.

"Who the hell is that?" She must have still been on a bullhorn setting because her outburst caught everyone's attention. Danato gave her a mortified glare. Ethan abruptly coughed into his hand. The sparkle in his eyes told her he was trying not to laugh. The businesswoman also turned to face her.

Her slender length was only accentuated by her hollow cheeks. Her bleached blond hair with dark roots gave her that "yeah, I dye it, so what?" look that some women enjoyed. The stick-straight hair twisted into a bun at the base of her scalp. The intentional flyaway strands gave her a casual, thrown together look, but Cori knew she had spent at least an hour getting them to all fly perfectly.

The woman smiled at her with a pleasant toothy—but not too toothy—smile. To top it off, the bitch had perfectly straight marshmallow-white teeth. Cori was about to plow the woman into the wall just for that slight.

Bleached hair and bleached teeth.

Cori must have been glaring at the woman pretty hard, because she lost her smile as quick as she gave it and turned away.

Something whirred in her ear, sending her eardrum into convulsions. She howled and pulled away from the tuning fork Belus held. He checked the number on the fork and made an X on his clipboard chart. He rewrote over the same X a couple more times, to get it good and noticeable on the paper.

He had already made three other marks, which she hadn't noticed him checking. She got the impression that whatever that fork had done to her; it wasn't good for her ear.

She looked back at the threesome, but they were gone. She caught sight of a red suit and fishnet stockings stepping through the exit door. Cori caught her eye again. She smiled and waved as she slipped out of sight.

Cori instinctively waved back. She didn't even know who the woman was. She had no reason to be so rude or judgmental about her. On the other hand, she was taller than her, skinnier than her, and prettier than her.

Bitch.

"Where are they going?" Cori said. Belus smiled and placed one finger on her lips. He mouthed, "Wait."

After two quiet tuning forks, she heard the distant hum of the third. "I hear..." She changed her voice to a low volume. "...something." He did the same to the other ear.

"How's that?" Belus said in a normal volume.

"Much better." She poked her fingers in her ears and wiggled out an itch that she couldn't actually scratch. "So what's with the skirt?"

Belus held up one finger while he finished marking his chart. He may as well have asked her to hold her breath under water, as anxious as she was to find out the answer. "The cochlear nerve is very sensitive to the time bubble. Which makes sense since it is basically—"

"That's very interesting," she interrupted. "Did you notice that woman in the red skirt suit that was talking to my... our... people?"

Belus nodded and looked over to where they had been. He must not have realized they had left already. "How was the wizard world?" He gave her a smug smile. He seemed to understand the hellish boredom she had just been through.

"Belus! Who was that woman?" She spoke slowly so he could understand her.

"Let me walk you home," he said as he slipped off his chair.

"I don't want to go home. I want to go wherever the other three went."

"Sorry kid, that's a private meeting." He closed the box and slipped the paperwork into an envelope taped to the top of it.

"What are they meeting about?"

"Come on, we'll talk after you've had a drink." He headed to the door.

"I don't want a drink." She pouted.

"Then we'll talk after *I* have a drink."

16

WITHOUT MUCH CHOICE, CORI followed Belus home. She stepped through the front door and left it open for him as she hung up her coat. She looked back and saw him standing patiently just outside the door. "Were you raised in a barn?"

"You have to invite me in." Cori stared at him a moment, not sure if he was just being polite to wait for an invitation or literal. "No, seriously, I can't enter until you invite me."

Her mouth dropped open. "Like a vampire?"

"No, not like that."

"Oh my God, are you a leprechaun?" she blurted out before establishing some relevancy for the accusation.

Belus lowered his eyelids, mostly hiding the eye roll he gave her. "No, just a dwarf, but I don't live here and the house has certain properties that don't allow unwelcome guests."

"I guess goblins don't count." Cori paused. "So what do I—"

"Just say, come in!"

"Come in." She threw the words at him like a hot potato from bare hands.

Belus stepped inside and shut the door. "Burr! Never have and never will get used to being cold to the bone." He hung up his coat and headed into the living room. "Alright, time for a drink."

"I don't think Danato keeps liquor here," she said just as Belus slid back a panel of wainscoting in the living room wall to reveal two shelves of liquor and glasses. She smiled at the ingenious hiding spot. "I knew that man had to be a drinker."

"Danato doesn't drink a lot, but he is a connoisseur of fine, hard liquors. Not one bottle in this collection is under one hundred dollars, and there is even one that is nearly eight hundred. That's the one you can't see. Invisible bottle." That statement notwithstanding, Cori still tried to see the un-seeable bottle. "I don't advise partaking in that one. He has been nursing that for 17 years."

Belus poured himself a sip of dark rum while Cori slipped off her shoes and settled in on the couch. "Care to try one?" Belus waved his hand to display the array of bottles to choose from.

Cori shrugged. "You pick."

"Hmm, what does a woman drink when she is rearing for a catfight?" He glanced at her with a playful, almost flirtatious smile.

She grinned at him. Almost simultaneously, they said, "Tequila!"

Cori laughed as he poured her a bit more than a sip of tequila. "I feel bad. I should be serving you. You're my *invited* guest."

"Oh, don't worry about it. I used to live here once upon a time. The house just doesn't remember all that."

"Where do you live now? You don't live in the prison, do you?"

He handed her the drink and sat down in Danato's usual chair. He looked miniscule in the big chair. "No, I have a small cottage off the northeast side of the prison. If the summer ever makes it back around, I'll have to invite you over for a barbeque."

"I'd like that." Cori sipped her tequila. She didn't know what good tequila was over bad tequila, but if strength was a measure, it was a very good tequila. "The east side? So is that off the old rainbow, near 5th and gold?"

"What?" he asked, confused by her quip. Cori slapped her knee as she mockingly guffawed at her leprechaun joke. "Oh, funny. No, it's on the corner of 5th and kiss-my-ass." He rolled the insult together, making it sound like a real name. Cori laughed for real. "I see someone is getting her sense of humor back. The bubble tends to leave you feeling a little off kilter; luckily you're on the fun half of the kilter."

"Either that or my alcohol is bypassing my liver," she said. Belus nodded and went back for another sip of rum. "So, what were we talking about before you forced me back to my home to drink really old liquor? Oh, yes, who's the leggy wish-she-were-blond?"

"Leggy?" Belus laughed.

"What's so funny about that?" Cori asked, offended that she wasn't getting in on the joke.

"It's a short-man joke." Belus brought back the bottle of tequila and poured her another sip even though she hadn't finished her first sip. He set the bottle on the coffee table and settled back into Danato's chair. "All dwarfs are leg men because the tits are too far away to enjoy."

Cori barked a laugh to show her appreciation. "I've never heard that before, that's good."

"No? How can you tell if a dwarf is looking at your eyes instead of your chest?"

"How?"

"He's not," Belus said flatly.

After a slight pause, Cori laughed hysterically. "I had no idea you were so funny," she said, wiping away a gleeful tear.

Belus shrugged. "You got to have a sense of humor about yourself otherwise someone will have it for you." He took a draw of his dark liquor, looking like he enjoyed the flavor, much like she might enjoy chocolate cake.

She smiled and sipped on hers as well. The taste was pungent, but the liquor was smooth and warming to her throat. She wasn't sure she could ever appreciate it the way Belus and Danato did, but she enjoyed being invited to the party. When she couldn't wait any longer, she asked the same question again. "So, about—"

"Oh, please don't ask again. I'm just coming to that." Belus took another sip, giving it a hasty swish before swallowing. He set his drink down and moved his full attention to her. "She is a liaison to the bigwigs on the board. The board of the prison is made up of a dozen or so high-ranking officials from across the world. We are the 'Area 51' of Russia." Belus air-quoted Area 51. "The board doesn't get together physically any more than they have to. If they meet twice in their own lifetime, that would be too much. So, instead they send out leggy blondes to do their correspondence work."

"What's her name?"

"Sophia, I think she said."

"You've never met her before?"

"Liaisons have a high turnover rate. It's not exactly a full-time job. By the time a need for one arises, the last one has already moved up in the ranks. I have my suspicions that they're using interns."

"Not a very secure practice."

"If they are interested in careers in high government, they might be the most secure option. Always choose the upwardly desperate when you want loyalty."

"What does she want with Ethan?" Cori sipped on her tequila since it was still in her hand.

"I'm not entirely sure. She didn't discuss anything with Danato first. We suspect that it has to do with the two competing resumes we sent to them for you and Ethan."

"Will they reject one?"

"Legally they can't. Everything that goes on in this place is seedy and underhanded, but believe it or not, we have a company handbook that identifies where and when to be seedy."

Cori nodded, strumming her fingers on her glass absent-mindedly.

"I'm sure it's nothing bad," he clarified.

"Why didn't she need to speak with *me*?" she asked, trying not to sound jealous.

Belus shrugged. "She just didn't." He stood up. "Anyway, rest up today. Recovering from a long stint in the time bubble can be a lot like jet lag with a hangover, especially the first time. We'll get back to a routine tomorrow." He finished his swill, put away the bottles, and headed to the door.

"Thanks, Belus," she said, holding up the drink.

He gave her a curt nod as he slipped on his coat and headed out.

Cori finished her liquor and took their glasses to the kitchen right away to wash them. She noticed Danato's bowl of muesli congealing on the table and picked it up on the way by.

She dumped the cereal down the garbage disposal and proceeded to wash the four pieces of dishware. She would never have thought about doing her dishes one at a time before living here, but the threat of goblins would turn anyone into a good housekeeper.

She noticed the box of chocolate cereal sitting on the counter beside her. She couldn't believe that a matter of hours ago—real time—she and Ethan had been fighting over chocolate puffs. It was also hard to believe that a matter of hours ago, time-bubble time, she was sitting in front of a fire, eating a worm heart, and contemplating whether she wanted to deflower Ethan.

She smiled at the thought. Her smile faded as a quick stab caught her in the back. "Knock it off!" She slapped herself over the shoulder.

She wanted to go back to the prison and burst in on "Lady Red's" meeting, but she knew Danato would have a fit. Besides, now that she knew the bitch was *somebody,* she knew she would at least have to fake being nice to her.

With visions of fishnet stockings and perfect teeth in her head, Cori slipped upstairs to shower and change her clothes. She may not have bleached teeth and perfectly chiseled legs, but she could at least have brushed teeth and shaved legs.

After her shower, Cori pulled her wet hair up in a hair tie and took a wild stab at being a warden's apprentice. She picked up a book from the coffee table she was supposed to be studying. She sat down on the couch and dove in with the concentrated aspiration of reading the words, understanding them, and remembering them.

Five minutes later, she threw the book back on the coffee table.

She wanted to throw something else, or punch something, but at the risk of offending the house, she didn't. A few more minutes of sulking brought her to only one logical conclusion. She picked up the book again and left.

E THAN SAT IN DANATO'S office in pure heaven. Sophie, a tall, beautiful blonde, stood next to him, fawning over his accomplishments at the prison. At any and every opportunity, she touched his arms or back. When she was excited about a particular feat of his, she would suck in air through her front teeth. She never stopped smiling, nor did she stop talking.

Danato seemed unimpressed by the whole display. He sat at his desk looking the part of the callous godfather. Ethan occasionally looked back at him, but no other expression was offered.

"You do such magnificent work here, Danato." Sophie again took another opportunity to touch Ethan, this time on his face. "It couldn't have worked out better for you. Too bad that dragon stuff isn't marketable. Customs would have a fit." Ethan smiled and nodded, feeling his face blush. He wasn't used to receiving so much attention from a woman, let alone such flamboyant enthusiasm. "I'm told that you have already completed your studies."

"Yes ma'am, every last book."

"Oh, don't call me ma'am. Ma'am is fine for mothers and old ladies, but not me. Call me Sophie."

"Okay, Sophie."

"That's better." She smiled and tugged on the sleeve of his shirt.

Ethan was suddenly aware that he had not changed clothes or showered in five days. He glanced over his dirty clothes and leaned his head down to do a half-assed sniff test. He wasn't a bouquet of roses, but he certainly wasn't toxic.

"Where was I?" Sophie said, pulling herself away from him.

"You were about to tell us why you're here," Danato announced firmly.

"Yes, I was about to tell you that." Sophie stepped in front of Ethan to take a seat beside him. He couldn't help but admire the view of her butt as it wiggled between him and Danato's desk. After she sat down, she put her hands on his legs. "We received the applications for two potential wardens, and we couldn't be happier. We were a little concerned about the other since she is female, but just because we haven't had a female warden doesn't mean we can't." Sophie waggled both her index fingers to "shame-shame" anyone who might think otherwise.

"We are fully expecting Ethan to excel in the competition," Danato interjected. "Cori is a bit behind in her research, and some of the more physical challenges may not be her shining point."

"You gave her a great recommendation, though," Sophie said.

"Yes, she has an accidental genius quality and natural survival instincts that just can't be denied."

"She sounds fabulous; I adore a woman who can think on her feet. That's why I've come here. We fully expect Ethan to do well in the competitions too, but win or lose, it may not change our interest in him." She winked at Ethan.

"Wait." Ethan looked back at Danato for confirmation. "You're not saying that I already have the job? Because Cori is working hard to compete for this. I want her to compete."

"No, no, I agree. She must compete." Sophie repositioned herself at the edge of her seat. "What we are saying is, there may be a place for you beyond the walls of this prison. If you win the competition and choose to take the warden's position, so be it. If you lose or decide not to take the position, we have another job opportunity waiting for you."

"Really? Outside of the prison?" He glanced at Danato. His gaze faltered at the suggestion, but he didn't object. Ethan had never considered leaving the prison. He was content to stay. He was proud to take over as warden for Danato. However, to be offered a job that allowed him to leave the prison was intriguing, to say the least.

"Yes, outside the prison," Sophie answered.

"Where would I be?"

Sophie laughed. "Everywhere and anywhere, you would be a world traveler. You would be in Paris one day and in Belize the next."

His mouth dropped. *Very* intriguing.

"It is the most exciting job on earth. You would be like a spy, only instead of killing people, you would be hunting creatures."

Ethan heard a snap. Danato's #2 pencil had become a victim of his thick fingers. A slight tick in his lip was the only change in the hard stare he directed at Sophie. Ethan looked back at her and caught a glimpse of her matching glare.

"Let's take a walk." Sophie smiled broadly back at him and stood up. "You should show me the facility. It's been a while for me." She linked her arm in his and they left the office without Danato.

18

CORI SAT INDIAN STYLE on the cold concrete floor, struggling to read the book on her lap. Cleos sat on the floor inside his cage with his back to her, leaning against the bars. He was a pale, gaunt man in his forties, with thick severe fingernails that bordered on being claws, but he was otherwise human. His dark chestnut hair was long, thinning, and lightly marbled with silver. It rested on his shoulders, begging to be put back in a ponytail. His narrow-slit eyes were accented with strong eyebrows. The trimmed Van Dyke goatee that he wore reminded Cori of vampires she had seen on television.

Despite his dark worldly quality, Cleos had been forceful in explaining he wasn't a blood-sucking bastardization of a human half-breed. That didn't stop her from keeping a safe distance from him while she interviewed him.

"According to this, you not only read people, but have the ability to make what you read from them come true.

Isn't that cheating?" she asked, holding her place in the book with her finger while she interrogated him.

Cleos scoffed. "I don't make anything come true, but on occasion, if my reading is powerful enough, the mind will make the event happen sooner than it was originally intended. It's kind of like a self-fulfilling prophecy."

"There's a formula in here for photophobia. Do I need to know that?"

Cleos tipped his head back and his eyes quivered under the lids. "No, but there are eight pages of questions on dietary habits, which will include the minimum prescribed amount of blood each photo-sensitive vampiric breed needs."

"Damn it. I don't suppose you could just tell me if I'm going to pass, so I can give up now?"

He looked back at her over his shoulder. "Not yet. You do understand I can't predict the future."

"But you just said..."

"I can predict future events based on my knowledge of the person and their surroundings. I get glimpses of a vague potential futures, but nothing is certain when the factors for the future lie outside of the person's control."

She looked up at him, crinkling her nose in confusion. "Then how do you know if these questions are on the test?"

"Because they haven't changed it in eighty years. Danato and Belus both took the same test as their fathers did."

"Belus took the warden test?"

"Yes, but he was turned down for his obvious physical maladies. The guards are all required to take the same test, but they don't have to score that well, and they don't get the option of the final exam."

She grimaced. "I repeat, how do you know if these questions are on the test?"

"Didn't you just read the chapter on my kind?" He glanced down at the book in her lap.

"Yes," she said as she closed the book and threw it at the bars, "but I can't understand it. That's why I'm here!" The book flopped back over to her and she slammed it on the ground once more to get the remainder of her statement across.

He stuck his hand out between the bars. She stared at it. "You want to know what I do? I'll show you."

"No, you're just going to eat me," she said flatly.

Cleos whipped around to face her. "I don't eat people. I'm a photophobe. When are you going to figure that out?" He grimaced, touching his stomach. "I hate vampires. They're... loud." Cori looked down the yellow-tinted hall at the irritated screeching blood suckers pressed to the doors of their cells. Each one was scrambling to grab her, even though she was too far out of reach. "I'll help you with the test, but under three conditions."

"Which are?" She arched an eyebrow in preparation for his demands.

"One: you never, ever equate me to a vampire again." Cori smirked, but nodded. "Two: you let me read you when you visit."

"Why?" she asked, narrowing her eyes.

"Because I'm bored, and it's kind of like having a cigarette."

She frowned at him, still not sure if she liked the idea of being someone's entertainment. "It's not like sex for you, is it?"

"No." He mirrored her disgust. "Sex is sex for everybody. Reading your mind would be what someone would do after sex. No, no, scratch that, bad image." He thought about it for a while. "Okay." He put his hands in a prayer position. "Reading people for me is like chocolate cake to you."

Cori felt a shiver down her spine. She scooted back from him. "I thought you said you had to touch me to read me. I was just thinking about chocolate cake today. How did you know that?"

"You really should have read my file before coming down here. I've already read you once, Corinthia. I can tell you your favorite flower, your first pet, and I can tell you the name of the first boy you kissed. Can you?"

Cori thought about her first kiss. She remembered what his lips tasted like and she remembered thinking his tongue shouldn't be in her mouth, and his name was… "I don't remember his name. How can you?"

"I can find anything in that pretty little head. Do we have a deal?" He paused, waiting for an answer. "Vince never would have brought you down here if he didn't trust me not to hurt you."

Cori lowered her eyes. "Okay, deal. What's the third thing?"

"Bring me some decent tea. These savages keep bringing me coffee."

She smiled. "What's wrong with coffee?"

"Besides being muddy pigswill? Consumerism, pesticides, and the debauchery of fair trade."

She laughed at his devotion to his pseudo-political stance.

She knew if Danato was there at that moment, he would list a thousand reasons not to associate with Cleos, but she needed help, and he wasn't asking for much. "Okay." She held out her hand. "Deal."

Cleos repositioned and cracked his knuckles. "I'm going to hand you something in your mind. It's just a tiny little memory. A good memory. It won't hurt you, but it will feel… weird."

She cringed as he reached out to touch her. He tapped her hand with one clawed finger. She looked down at her hand in case there might be some physical remnant of his offering on her hand. "I didn't feel–"

Then Cori screamed, or perhaps it was more of a "weeeee!"

She felt the floor drop out from under her and, for only a split second, she was falling. She recovered from the sensation and touched the floor to make sure it was still there. It was a terrifying feeling, but somehow a smile crept onto her face. Her heart was beating fast, and she was gulping for air. "What the hell was that?"

Cleos grinned ear to ear. "Did you like it?"

"No!" she said, matching her smile with a laugh.

"Are you sure you didn't like it just a little?"

She waved her finger at him. "That was nothing like chocolate cake."

Cleos put his arms above him, leaning into the bars. "It's like chocolate cake for me. It's like whatever you want it to be for you." He tipped his brow.

Cori shook her head, but couldn't wipe the smile from her face. "Okay, okay, I see how you could be dangerous... and addictive, but I still don't understand how you know the questions on the test."

"I've had my hands on numerous people in this prison. I'm not a high-security prisoner. Not a deadly threat. Hell, you're not the first fly in my web." Cleos danced his fingers over his imaginary web.

"Said the spider to the fly." Cori stood up. "I have to go study my zookeeper's manual. I might be back."

"You will be. With no one else to talk to, you'll eventually seek out my beneficial friendship."

She rolled her eyes before leaving, but didn't bother asking what that meant. Like he said, he couldn't read her future.

19

ETHAN WASN'T SURE WHEN the tour had stopped, but he found himself standing with Sophie amidst the aquariums. To be specific, he was standing and Sophie was leaning against the glass, drawing him in closer with every coy touch to his chest. He couldn't help but enjoy the attention.

"So, what is the job, exactly?" He spoke loudly to be heard over the water pumps.

"Just what I said." Sophie didn't bother speaking up, which forced him to lean in further to hear the answer. "You would hunt down the creatures that need to be housed in the prison."

"I thought the collectors handled that."

"No, they only track what we've already found. They are like rabid bloodhounds. They will find and collect anything we have a scent for, but until we have a scent, we need strong, cunning men."

Ethan finally gave in and put one arm on the aquarium behind her, leaving them very close. "What would I catch?"

"Whatever you can. This particular job is not only free from confinement, but you would be very, very well off."

"How well off?"

"Thousands for each easy catch, tens of thousands for troublesome finds, and... well, you get the picture."

"What's the catch?"

"No catch." She leaned forward to whisper in his ear. "Cash payment upon delivery. Danato will pay you himself, from his back pocket."

"This job is not contingent on my performance in the competition?"

She shook her head, wetting her already glistening lips. "As long as little miss is around to do this dirty work, you can take the job right now. I even brought papers to sign if you were so inclined."

"What happens if I sign them now?"

"You leave with me." She winked. "I get you set up in a nice flat somewhere in Europe, and in several days, you would receive your first assignment. Then off you hunt." She traced her hand down his chest and stomach. Her finger caught on his waistband before falling away.

He could feel the heat of her body so close. He wanted to go in for a kiss, but it seemed inappropriate even after her obvious invitations.

Just as he was about to move away, he remembered Cori chastising him for not taking advantage of opportunities. He changed his surrender to attack and went for her lips.

He expected her to turn her cheek or at least push him away after a few seconds, but she did no such thing. She kissed him back with the same vigor. She latched her leg into the crook of his knee and combed her fingers through his hair.

He had never kissed a woman so passionately. He pushed morality and common decency to the wayside. Every yearning he had suppressed over the last year came back to him in a frenzied flood.

He lifted Sophie off the floor. She moaned with appreciation and wrapped her legs around him. He pushed against her, sliding his hand up her skirt. He had no intention of stopping. A quick tug on her panties and a downed zipper were the only two steps left in this puzzle. It would be quick and finally over with. Even if the experience provided nothing to Sophie, he knew she would pretend to enjoy it.

If not for a flicker in his peripheral vision, he would have thrown Sophie to the floor and taken those last two steps without hesitation. He surfaced from his lip-lock to look at what had distracted him.

"Cori," he said, still pressing Sophie into the aquarium behind them. He choked a laugh and smiled through the rouge of his warming cheeks. He cleared his throat and released Sophie. "Sorry, I didn't see you there."

He let Sophie adjust her skirt before moving away from her. For his part, he didn't need to wait. He had cooled as fast as he had heated.

Cori stood frozen, just staring at him. Her face was a blank slate waiting for someone to hand her a cue card for which emotion to project.

"So, you're Cori," Sophie said, adjusting her hair. "I'm Sophie; I've heard so many good things about you."

Cori looked down at her book as if it might hold some explanation within its pages about what she had just witnessed. "I was just doing some hands-on studying," she said, dazed. "I have to go over the dietary... animals..." she trailed off.

"We were just discussing job options for Ethan," Sophie said.

Ethan watched Cori's face come back from the dazed stupor like her hypnotist had called out the secret word to her awakening. "What job options?"

Sophie motioned for him to reveal what he wanted.

"I have an opportunity to leave the prison. I can take a job hunting the creatures we house here."

"You wouldn't be the warden?" Cori asked.

"No, you would." He smiled, hoping that would draw some enthusiasm from her, but it didn't. "I would just be a delivery boy."

"How often would you come back?"

Ethan looked at Sophie. He hadn't asked that question. He hadn't thought of that question.

"Several times a year," Sophie said.

"A year?" Cori's voice cracked on the word.

He could see she didn't like that answer. "This isn't set in stone." He took a step toward her, away from Sophie. "What do you think of it?"

"What do *you* think?" Cori threw the question back at him, unanswered.

"I think it's an *opportunity* I should consider."

Her face cringed. "You should..." Cori looked back at Sophie. A glare spread across her face. "You should do whatever feels right."

Ethan watched her face harden, as if every emotion she had ever felt had gotten hog-tied and stuffed in a cage beside her heart. "Is that all you have to say?" He hated to bait her, but he didn't want to feel bad about wanting to leave the prison. He didn't want to feel guilty for wanting to be with a woman that wanted him. He did, however, want Cori to feel something about that: anger, sadness, something. He wanted a reaction, some kind of proof that she gave a damn. He wanted proof that he had a shot with her.

"Yes." She hissed the word at him before hugging her book and trudging away.

He watched her leave. She may not have had any emotions to offer the situation, but he was holding a myriad of sentiments: guilt, anger, frustration, anticipation. Mostly, though, he just felt sick. Looking back at Sophie's grinning face, he couldn't imagine why, two minutes ago, he couldn't keep his hands off her.

CORI STORMED AWAY FROM the scene, not wanting to show her tears. She couldn't believe, after the time they had shared in the wizard world, that within an hour he would paw a woman he just met.

Away from them both, she threw her book and fell to her knees. She could sense her sorrow demon taking a tight grip over her again, but she couldn't do anything to stop it. She could only sob and wonder how different things might have been if she had only tried to kiss him a second sooner. One damn second.

"I'M NOT SAYING YOU can't do the job." Danato brandished his pasta spoon at Ethan. The plastic pronged spoon still held a wet noodle that flapped with every jab. He was preparing his famous "spaghetti à la steak." One of Ethan's favorites, but again, served way too often.

Ethan set out the plates and flatware on the table while keeping a good distance between him and Danato's wielded utensils. Cori finished sprinkling her last layer of cheese on the cheesy bread, which she would follow with oregano and bake to a crispy, melted perfection. Another of Ethan's favorites, one he had not tired of.

Cori had yet to say two words to him, not counting the "excuse me" she'd said to get around him to the fridge earlier. He couldn't tell if she was more mad or sad, but he was certain that if she looked him in the eyes, he would know for sure. Unfortunately, she was avoiding eye contact as staunchly as conversation.

"Why wouldn't I take it?" he asked, still not seeing the catch to Sophie's proposal.

"Because you will die!" Danato's voice boomed through the house. Behind him, Cori jumped from the outburst. With her back to the stove, she couldn't see the transformation in Danato's face that always preceded his arcs in temper.

Ethan had long since become immune to Danato's dramatic rage, but he still hated being in the path of it when it came barreling out of him. "How is that not saying I can't do the job?"

Cori moved to Danato and touched his shoulder. For a split second, Ethan thought she was going to offer mediation to his case, but instead, she moved him out of her way to place her cheesy bread in the oven.

"I'm not saying you *can't* do the job. I'm saying the job is too dangerous for you to do. That's not based on my opinion, or my evaluation of your skill, it is based on statistical analysis of past hunters."

"I get it. It's dangerous," Ethan said snidely.

Danato drew his spaghetti-spoon revolver so fast the half-cocked weapon shot a noodle onto Ethan's shirt. "Don't be blithe to me, boy."

"Will you help me here, Cori?" Ethan asked, approaching the island.

Cori looked up from her trance on the stove timer. She reached over, removed the noodle from his shirt, and tossed it in the sink.

Ethan looked her up and down. "That's all you have to offer to this situation?" He didn't know how her sad and mad were balancing out, but *his* mad was tipping the scales.

"If you want an opinion on your job prospects, why don't you ask your new girlfriend?"

"Girlfriend?" Danato eyed Ethan from the other side of Cori.

"Yup." Cori reached in front of Danato and pulled the pasta off the stove. Danato had a tendency to make mushy pasta, so Cori always watched the time for him. She moved it to the sink and dumped the pot's contents into a colander. "They were pretty close this afternoon," she said with her back to them. "At least they chose the right level—with the animals."

"What's this about?" Danato's eyes darted between the two, searching for the answers.

Ethan pulled a serving platter out of the cupboard above the fridge and handed it to Danato for his steaks. "Nothing happened," he said with wide eyes and clear pronunciation. He moved up behind Cori. She finished returning the pasta back to the big pot. "Nothing happened," he announced directly to her, in case she hadn't heard him say it to Danato.

She ripped herself away from her pasta to face him. "That was nothing? If nothing more happened, it was only because I interrupted!" She tried to walk away, but he backed up and blocked her way between the fridge and the island.

"I recall being chastised the last time I let an opportunity like that go." He intended to sound sarcastic, but his voice dripped with animosity.

She shook her head and took the long way around the island. "That's not opportunity," she snapped.

He went after her, but Danato blocked his way. "Easy."

"Oh, for the love of God, stop treating her like a porcelain doll. She can take care of herself." The timer dinged on the cheesy bread. Danato removed the bread while Ethan took the short way to the table. "Do you have something to say to me?" he asked, paralleling Cori's movement from the opposite end of the table.

Cori shifted uncomfortably under his gaze, but didn't speak. She started collecting the plates off the table.

Ethan glanced at Danato, who was stacking his steaks on the platter. He moved to the side of the table and blocked his face from Danato. He leaned down on the table and tried to convey urgency in a quiet voice. "Do you have anything to say to me about... anything? The job? Sophie? Me?"

Ethan saw the emotions behind her eyes, but for some reason, she didn't want to let them out. Fear, resentment, grief, whatever it was, it was preventing her from letting him in. Ethan eased away from the table, barely able to think past his disappointment in her. He helped her pick up the silverware and napkins he had just put out.

"What are you doing?" Danato yelled, suddenly aware of their actions. "We haven't eaten yet!"

"I'm not hungry," Cori said, already taking a step from the table, waiting for any excuse to bolt.

"I made steak!" Danato yelled. She was still again. "We are eating dinner." Danato placed the steak-filled platter on the edge of the island.

They started reassembling the table, silently adding the steaks and the cheesy bread. They both sat down opposite each other, placing their napkins while they waited for Danato to finish the pasta.

Ethan stared at Cori, waiting for an answer, a comment, a lethal defensive tactic, anything. "Say something to me? I'm right here. I'm listening. I would like to know if anything that has happened today has affected you adversely."

"Aside from almost hurling at seeing you paw a woman you just met?" she mumbled, keeping her eyes away from him.

"I'm not going to apologize for that, Cori."

She glanced up at him. She must have needed to see the determination in his face before she could believe his statement.

Danato sat down with the pasta pre-mixed with sauce. "That *is* rather inappropriate, Ethan," Danato said tentatively.

"It *was* inappropriate," Ethan admitted. "I shouldn't have participated in such a public display, but I won't apologize for the encounter. It was consensual. I was only responding to her signals, which she made *very clear*."

"I'm sure her signals have been honed over many, many encounters." Cori spooned her spaghetti on her plate and shoved the bowl at him.

He took the bowl and did likewise. "Say what you want about her *experience*. At least there's no room for error. No eggshells to walk over. No baggage to help carry. Not to mention she just says what she's thinking... out loud!"

Cori dropped her fork and rolled back her shoulders. Ethan wondered if her sorrow demon had been bothering her since the afternoon's incident. "You want to know what I think? I think she is just using you to get you to join her hunting squad. She's manipulating you."

"Well, at least she's manipulating me to give me freedom, instead of me manipulating her for it." He tipped his head, glaring his full meaning at her.

She stared back at him. Her mouth dropped open for a moment, but she closed it.

Ethan regretted the statement the instant he said it. She had admitted to influencing Vince in the time bubble.

She had presented it as an olive branch to help explain her actions. In return, he weaponized that olive branch and used it to hurt her. And hurt her, it did.

Cori threw her napkin down and shoved her chair out, prepared to bolt again.

"I made steak," Danato stated with the implication that she stay at the table. He didn't foist many agendas on them at home, but he held the evening meal sacred.

She reluctantly pulled her chair back to the table and played with her food.

Ethan wanted to catch her eye, so he could mouth, "*I'm sorry*" to her, but she kept her face down on her plate. With a soft voice laced with self-deprecation, he asked, "Why would you even want me to stay? All we do is argue."

"Who said I wanted you to stay?" she pointed out. Ethan's heart clenched at the statement. He caught sight of a drop falling into her food, a salty tear that he had caused.

"Here, I thought that bubble would make things better," Danato said between bites. "It only seems to have intensified the emotions behind the arguing. Is that all you did in the bubble?" Danato looked between the two for his answer.

"No," Ethan said, clearing his throat. "We didn't argue as much there."

"I think I should have left you both in there a hair longer," Danato said. "Maybe that would pop this festering zit of hate."

Ethan dropped his fork onto his plate, and Cori followed suit. The graphic metaphor had taken the edge off whatever was left of their hunger.

21

AFTER DINNER, THEY BOTH attempted to look occupied, all the while waiting to leave the room. Danato, unaffected by the tension, was happily off to sleep with his newspaper blanket. When Cori finally tossed her book on the coffee table and stretched, Ethan commented on how late it was.

He let Cori head upstairs first. He followed her after he removed Danato's glasses and set them on the coffee table. When he got to her door, she was already inside. He knocked and tried the doorknob. As he'd expected, it was locked.

He heard a scuffle inside, then silence. He knocked again, slightly louder. Nothing.

"Cori, open the door. I'm not leaving until you do." Nothing. "I'm sorry, house. Please forgive me." Ethan stepped back and kicked the door in.

Cori yelped, jumping off her couch and backing away from the splintered entryway. Ethan listened downstairs for Danato's snores before coming inside and shutting the door behind him.

He looked around the living room setup that mimicked his own—except with feminine touches. Plush, colorful pillows on a taupe couch, with traditional wooden end tables instead of his modern plastic ones. Much like his living room, the only thing missing was the flat screen television to give the couch a purpose.

Cori hung back by her far end table, still in shock at his bold entrance. "What the hell, Ethan?"

"I see you got your apartment, finally."

She looked around the room as if seeing it for the first time. "Yeah, she forgave me. That doorframe had better go against you, though."

Ethan looked back at the splintered frame. He was surprised it hadn't held up better, given the magical nature of the house. It was just like any other door, only as strong as the doorjamb.

He turned back to her and took a step toward her. She took a step away from him. He clenched his jaw and raised a scolding finger to her. "Don't, don't do that. Don't back away from me like I'm some horrible monster that should be penned up in that prison." He slashed his thumb back in the general direction of the prison.

Cori stepped forward, meeting him at a sober conversational distance. "Why did you just knock down my door?"

"Because I'm done with the silent treatment. I need you to talk to me."

"And tell you what, Ethan? You want me to lay out emotions that stem from territorial instincts that I don't have the right to have?" She slapped her chest. "I get it Ethan. Enter hot blonde, who isn't emotionally traumatized by fear and grief. Add pent-up sexual frustration, and flirting, and voilà. Inappropriate, sure, but understandable."

Ethan exhaled a breath he hadn't realized he was holding. "Thank you for understanding that, at least." He stepped away to examine her furniture. "I need to talk to you about the job."

"I can't make that decision for you."

"And I can't make it without you," he said with more intensity than he intended. "I need your permission. I was the one left behind last time, and it hurt like hell. I need to know you can live with this decision."

She crossed her arms. "Sounds like you've already made up your mind."

"My mind is made up, but my feet will stay firmly planted until you push or pull me." He watched her react to the prospect of choosing his path. When he didn't see the realization he wanted, he continued. "There is only one thing that will keep me here, and it can't be hope."

Her eyes met with his. She looked like a deer caught in headlights, stunned into submission by blinding honesty.

"I don't mean that to sound like an ultimatum," he continued, "but I'm sick of trying to define this relationship. I want more. I want whatever it was I felt with Sophie this afternoon."

She looked away, deep in thought. Her eyes wavered back and forth, as if she was reading her own thoughts off a belated memo from her brain.

"No more, Cori." Ethan stalked over to pull her out of her internal discussion. He took her shoulders gruffly, but with controlled pressure in his grip. "Come out of that brain of yours and talk to me. Tell me what you're thinking and feeling." He took down one shaking hand and placed it over her heart. His fingers brazenly skirted her breasts. He fought against his baser instincts to keep his hands and eyes from roaming.

She looked at him somberly. Her heart thumped against his hand, and her chest rose and fell with each breath, slowly coming to terms with the proximity of his body. "I think you should take the job."

He sank away from her, dropping all physical contact. It was what he expected, and partially what he wanted, but it felt like a hot knife had plunged into his heart. He backed up a couple more steps, searching for something to say so he could exit with dignity.

"I feel..." she continued. He looked up, realizing she wasn't finished. "My heart..." Her voice caught. "...will break when you leave. The very instant you are out of sight, my sorrow demon will gorge."

"Why would you ask me to go, then?"

"Because if you don't leave, you'll always wonder. My decision will have made you a prisoner to me, and this place. You should go be just you for a while. I'll be here. I'm not going anywhere." She gave a fleeting smile. "I need you to choose, too. I need you to choose me for me, and not by default."

He wanted to hold her. To show her he had long ago made his choice.

"You have my blessing, Ethan. Get the hell out of this place."

Ethan let all the unpleasant emotions drain off him. This was, ultimately, what he wanted. He wanted to say something to mark the moment. His mind rallied, spurring him to profess his love. He pushed back the incessant aspiration and moved to her door.

"I'll let Sophie know our decision." Even as he walked out the door to his separate apartment, he noted how good it felt to say *our*. They had finally agreed on something. Ironically, it was through their conjoined effort that they had decided to separate.

22

Danato awakened Cori early the next morning. She didn't question his motives for the early rise. She just pulled herself out of bed and got dressed. When she checked her hair in the mirror, she noticed the dip in her left shoulder.

Yesterday had fed her sorrow demon well. His fat little belly was weighing her down. She tried to lift her shoulder to balance her gait, but the determined little bastard wasn't budging. She ignored it, pulled her hair back, and went down to have breakfast.

Instead of breakfast, Danato threw her overstuffed down coat into her face. "Hey!" Her muffled cry went unnoticed as snow boots, gloves, and a scarf followed the coat. "What the bugger is wrong with you?"

"We have to go now, or we'll miss him."

She threw on her boots and coat, still not understanding the urgency. Danato pulled her out the door even as she zipped up her coat.

They ran to the prison and through the main foyer, down to the loading docks. She arrived panting. Danato wasn't nearly as winded, but he grasped at his leg and immediately sought out a crate to sit on.

The loading crew was running like a well-oiled machine this morning. Crates containing absolutely nothing were nailed tightly with nail guns. They loaded each one into the outgoing truck with a forklift, despite the lack of contents.

Sophie was amid the bustle. Her winter attire—plucked straight out of Doctor Zhivago—accentuated her features as well as her business suit. She was unnecessarily cheery, as usual, offering Cori a strumming finger wave.

Sophie stood next to a man wearing a full-length gray felt coat and a 1950s-style fedora. With his back to her, Cori assumed the man was a new arrival and was the cause for her imperative morning jog.

As he turned, she saw the young face peek from beneath the hat brim. *Ethan* and Sophie were rather the duo in their high fashion. Cori finally understood the pressing situation.

Ethan saw her and strolled over. Sophie came right along with him.

"Leaving so soon?" Cori asked.

"The sooner the better," Sophie jibed. "Just kidding, Danato." Sophie created an awkward threesome, standing nearly between Cori and Ethan. After a brief moment of silence, Sophie elbowed Ethan. "Well, for goodness' sake, hug your friends goodbye. You won't see them for at least a few months."

Ethan leaned over to Sophie. "Would you mind giving me a minute?" He smiled warmly.

"Sure thing." Sophie's eyes almost disappeared with her grin. She walked away, calling directions to the loaders on where to put her luggage.

Ethan gave Cori an amused smile and wide eyes, suggesting he knew what a nut she was. Before either of them could say anything, Danato hobbled over to replace Sophie in the threesome.

Ethan extended his hand to shake. Danato used it to pull him in for a hug. Cori could see him wince as Danato hugged a little too generously.

"You always have a job here, and a home." Danato slapped his back firmly. "Don't forget that."

Ethan pulled away and nodded. Both men locked their jaws, as if they were struggling to bite back further sentiments. "Thank you, Danato," Ethan finally said after a moment to compose himself, "for everything." He paused. "Everything," he stated again, since he couldn't pick just one debt to illustrate his gratitude.

Unlike Sophie, Danato knew when to leave them alone. Instead of heading back to his crate, he left the loading docks entirely.

Ethan looked around to make sure no one else needed to say goodbye to him. He finally turned his attention to her.

"You're an idiot to take this job," she said, trying to lighten the mood. "You could stay here in a cushy, upper management job, but instead you choose to be a peon and do dangerous bounty hunting."

"Where was this argument last night?" he asked with the tinge of a smile.

"Are you kidding? I would do anything to get this job. I'm just saying you are a complete sap for falling for my dastardly plot of corporate ladder-climbing."

"So, you've won again. How do you do that?"

"I think it's my dumb luck."

"Hmmm, didn't we decide the PC word was *clever*?" His smile filled in as he stepped forward. "You know I won't be back for a while. Don't you think you could have given me something more to remember you by than a tousled ponytail and dark-circled eyes?" Cori smiled even as she feigned a glare. "A little makeup; at least acknowledge your hairbrush exists."

She jabbed him in the stomach. "I just woke up. I have ChapStick." Cori pulled the balm from her coat pocket and applied it with a "ta-da" motion to follow. "How's that?"

"Much better. It really completes the ensemble."

"Ethan, chop chop!" Sophie hollered from the freight truck. He didn't look back at her.

"I didn't know you were leaving right away."

"Things progressed rather chaotically last night after I talked to Sophie. She was insistent." He rolled his eyes. "Cori, I want you to know that... the way I feel..."

"...shouldn't interfere with your time away from here." She understood what he wanted to say, but he needed to act without reference to those feelings for a change. "You should forget about me and this place while you're away. You should have fun. Get drunk. Get laid. Whatever!" Cori laughed. "I just mean that if you've only ever met one fish, how do you know you even like fish?"

Ethan furrowed his brow. "I'm pretty sure I like fish."

She shrugged and nodded to Sophie. "Maybe you like sharks better."

"Wow, I'm impressed. You didn't use the more catty *blowfish* euphemism."

She wasn't aware of when his hand had become entangled in hers, but their fingers were dancing with each other, caressing and tickling in a way that made the outside world slip away. Though she had held his hand before, she had never really felt it. His skin was callused, but not rough.

His smile had long since faded, along with hers. Their eyes were locked, stopping all time. He stepped in, closing the last of the breathable space between their bodies.

"You're a better catch than you think you are," he said, sticking to her fish metaphor.

He started to back away, but something stopped him. His hand stopped fidgeting in hers, and he locked his fingers in hers. He leaned in without hesitation and kissed her.

She could tell he intended to give her a nice chaste kiss with just a hint of wetness that could be interpreted as a friendly goodbye. However, once his lips hit hers, he nibbled in a little further, taking in a little more lip with each subtle reposition.

His hand tightened on her fingers as he parted his lips for a deeper kiss. His tongue barely teased her lip. She resisted the urge to offer her own. Just as she got a taste of his freshly brushed minty mouth, his lips clamped for a final forceful aching suckle before he drew away.

Their eyes locked again, unable to pass off the kiss as anything less than carnal. Not even the jog over had made Cori's heart beat so fast. She could see in his face the same disappointment that she was feeling. She wanted to replay the scene she had witnessed yesterday, with her in place of Sophie. She knew he wanted that, too.

The heat between them didn't readily fade, even as Sophie's insistent chirp begged for Ethan's attention. "Coming," he hollered back, not releasing Cori's eyes. "Say the word," he whispered to her.

She knew what he meant. *Stay.* One simple word and he would walk away from that dock with her instead of Sophie. One word and they could race back home and hole up in a room, making love until every ounce of hungry desire was satiated.

For a moment, she almost thought she would say it, but she couldn't. As much as it hurt her not to, he still needed to leave. He needed to see what the world had to offer. She didn't have a chance in hell winning out over the whole world, but that was the risk she had to take.

She licked her lips, trying to take in a little more of his taste before speaking. "Go." Her lip trembled after she said it.

His disappointment shifted into shock, but it only lasted a moment. A stern determination settled in his eyes. His hand slipped from hers, and he stepped away.

He climbed the steps to the platform and jumped on board the truck with only a cursory glance back. He disappeared into the back to stash himself with the rest of the cargo. The doors shut and Cori felt her neck tighten as her shoulder pulled down further, bearing the weight of her sorrow demon.

The truck rumbled to life and drove away. She watched it go, just to make sure it didn't have any unexpected drop-offs. No such luck, dumb or otherwise.

She strolled out of the loading dock and stopped outside the door. Danato was leaning against the wall in the hallway. He looked up, apparently waiting for her. She hadn't intended to, but she broke into tears at the sight of him. He moved to her and embraced her. She grabbed onto him as tightly as she could and cried until her sorrow demon was full to the brim.

23

"**M** M-HMM."

Cori had been sitting beside the short, bald, pointy-nosed businessman for over an hour. He looked like a used-car salesman in his cheap brown suit and bow tie. His hairy, gnarled fingers thrummed the red binder in his lap. With each successive "mm-hmm" he made a new mark in his notes. Despite Danato's shining review of her performance, the man had only said "mm-hmm" about thirty times.

She peeked over to read his papers, but they were all in shorthand, which she couldn't read. Giving up the effort to please him, she slumped back in her chair and propped her feet up on the desk. Danato glared at her audacity, but she ignored him. There would be no more sucking up today.

Mr. Nose, as Cori had designated him when she forgot his name, shifted his spectacles, and pursed his lips as if his tongue were searching for the last vestiges of lunch in his front teeth. He scribbled down a few more things, after which he turned his critiquing gaze to her. He perused her as if he might see the redeeming qualities that Danato had spoken of.

"According to *my* records," Mr. Nose recited like an IRS agent, "Corinthia has several offenses to her name."

She didn't like her name on his lips, especially her full name. It somehow felt violating to her for him to use it when Danato had clearly introduced her as Cori.

"Such as?" Danato leaned back and waited for the recitation.

"I understand there was an incident involving the death of a merman." Mr. Nose crinkled his nose before rubbing away the itch he couldn't adequately scratch in company.

"She was defending herself," Danato said.

"After she put herself in danger," Mr. Nose was quick to point out.

"She was reprimanded and punished," Danato clarified.

"What about injuring that transmorph?" Mr. Nose went on.

"That was the best thing to happen to my prison in eight years." Danato glanced at her. She bit back a smile. She wanted to defend herself, but she liked watching Danato do it for her.

"*My* records show..." Mr. Nose began.

"Stop saying 'my records,' you arrogant ass!" Danato thundered. "Those are my reports you're reading. If I had not been so forthcoming to report all those incidents, you would have no *records*. Did you read the part about her trapping a goblin with a prism? Have you gotten my report about the wizard bubble yet? Cori has shown significant instinct at this prison. Some of it may have been initiated by foolhardiness, but it has all been useful." Danato took a deep breath after getting out everything he wanted to say.

"All well and good, but..." Mr. Nose examined Cori as if she were a bug crawling on his food. "She is hardly in physical condition to complete the application process."

"I can kick your ass," she mumbled.

"I'm sure you can." Mr. Nose smiled with tensed lips. "However, I am not a dragon, am I?" His brow tipped and his smile turned to a sneer.

"What did you come here to do?" Danato asked, drawing himself forward to lean on his desk again.

"I came to evaluate this woman for a position that is far more important than simply a whim."

"I've been working my butt off for this. I have had my head in a book every night for the last..." Cori reflected on the six months that had passed since she returned to the prison. She couldn't believe the weeks since Ethan had left could now be measured in months.

"Cori has every right to apply for the job," Danato jumped in. "If she passes, she'll have proved her worth and she can take the job. If she doesn't, we can get Ethan back."

"Sophie was a little quick to take Ethan. She shouldn't have." Mr. Nose sniffled and rubbed his nose again, still trying to alleviate his itch. "He is an excellent bounty hunter, but the board cannot accept your recommendations to have Cori as an applicant to the warden position."

Danato was simmering nicely on the angry side, but he didn't blow up, as Cori had suspected he would. Her temper, on the other hand, was beyond boiling. "What a flippin crock!" She dropped her feet and stood up. "Is this a woman thing?"

Mr. Nose also stood, tucking his portfolio in the crook of his arm. "No," he said flatly. "This is a pain-in-the-ass thing. You are one. We don't like that. We need someone in charge that will be compliant with our rules and regulations. Right, Danato?"

Cori waited for steam to come out of Danato's ears. His face was slightly red, and his jaw was set tight, but he didn't say a word. He locked on her pleading eyes, but there was nothing in his face to suggest he had an argument for Mr. Nose.

"Oh, don't look at him, Miss Reiger. Whether he's admitted it to you or himself, he has always known that we would never give someone as volatile as you the reins to this facility."

She gave up on Danato and stepped toe to toe with Mr. Nose. "You're right, Mr. Nose," she said, not bothering to recollect his given name. "I have no intention of being compliant. That is not in my nature, but none of the 300-plus prisoners housed in this facility are submissive. They aren't going to follow your rules and regulations either. So, if you want someone to do things by the book, then bring Ethan back. I have no intention of being anyone's lapdog."

She threw a glance at Danato. She could tell he wasn't happy about the implication, but she didn't care. She had just wasted five months working toward a goal that she had no chance of achieving.

She stomped to the door and threw it open. Two steps through the frame, her chest radiated hot pain. She felt her body lift as she was thrown backwards through the air twelve feet. It would have been farther, but the back wall of Danato's office stopped her, sending her into the black of oblivion.

24

DANATO PUSHED BACK THOUGHTS of strangling the little twerp before him. Despite what Cori may have thought, he'd had no idea the board would outright refuse her application. He was just as furious as she was, and he intended to fight to get her reconsidered. This pencil-pusher wasn't the only person he could appeal to on the board.

Cori was on her way to the door before he could explain. He stood to call her back. His mouth opened just as the door did.

A familiar blue glimmer just outside the door stopped his voice.

Lightning.

The bolt shot into Cori faster than he could react. She was thrown like a ragdoll against the back wall. The sheetrock dented from the impact and ejected dust into the air. She hit the floor, limp and motionless.

"Cori!" he yelled before his body constricted. Waves of electricity crawled around his body like tentacles. Out of the corner of his eye, he saw the face of his attacker.

Efrat.

The elementals were out.

Danato's eyes glazed and he passed out.

Sometime later, Danato woke in the gym. The thick walls muted the prison sirens. The oversized halogen lights were at half power, indicating their energy reserves were being siphoned into the security system. He was tied up on the floor, along with every other guard in the prison. They looked like a refugee camp: wounded, and worried.

Mr. Godfrey, the pencil-pusher from the board, wasn't far from him, struggling futilely against his restraints. The irritating man flopped on his belly like a fish. "You call this a secure prison?" he fumed when he saw Danato was awake.

Danato rolled his eyes. "This happens at least yearly, Mr. Godfrey. That's why I'm here."

"Just my luck that it happened on my visit," Godfrey whined.

"Not luck. They planned it for your arrival. We were all distracted. Any time I am gone or thoroughly occupied, they attempt an escape."

"Attempt? They are out!"

"Not yet." Danato shook his head. "We're in lockdown. They would be out of the building if they could."

"Who exactly are *they*?" Godfrey asked.

"The elementals," he answered, but Godfrey only crinkled his nose in confusion. "Don't you have them in your reports?" Danato mocked.

"I don't remember them all."

"You will remember them now. They are the top level: Efrat, Remi, Hirem, and Garr. They are our problem children, if children were ego-centric psychopaths with a desire to destroy the world."

"I don't remember anything about the top level in my reports."

"Maybe you don't have that much clearance." Danato stilled him with a hard stare. "They are under military contract. They should have been destroyed long ago."

Danato heard heavy footsteps approach. The metal straps on Garr's black leather boots rattled from the concussive landing of each long stride. The rest of his outfit—strictly black—was teeming with metal hoops and tabs, necessary as finger-holds and grips. His pale skin, made paler by the outfit, bore no scars or defects. He was a life-sized porcelain doll, maniacal and completely nuts, but beautiful. Except for his head of loose brilliant blond curls, he had no body or facial hair.

He stopped beside Danato and crouched down to speak to him. "Tsk, tsk, I bet you didn't expect this today." His words strained through rasping vocal cords, contradicted the softness of his face.

"Finally pooled your powers of evil together, did you?" Danato nodded to the other three elementals hovering by the entrance.

"Yes, we did. It's working well, so far. What do you think?" As if in a permanent state of Botox overdose, Garr's face only offered muted expressions. He couldn't manage a full smile, but Danato saw how pleased he was with the takeover.

"How many have you killed?" he asked, concerned about the other half of his team not currently hogtied with him.

"We didn't take pulses or anything, but eighteen are down for the count, including your lovely."

Danato tried not to think about Cori's crumpled body, bleeding to death on his office floor. "The lockdown will keep you here until help arrives," he said, refusing to entertain the elemental with his emotional rage over their actions.

"Help is hundreds of miles away. Do you really think we're worried about that? We have the entire prison, and there isn't a single person left standing to save the day."

CORI'S BODY *WAS* PAIN. So much pain. There were no muscles, nor bones, nor appendages; there was just one all-inclusive ache. Except her head. Above all the other pains, her head prevailed to offer a predominant throbbing migraine.

She raised her head just enough to look around.

She got a clear view of Danato's bottom desk drawer before she passed out again.

GARR GAVE DANATO A hard slap on his bicep, a mocking comfort for his irrefutably sucky day. He could hear the singe and smell the burned fabric, but Garr removed his hand before the heat became too intense. He glanced at the smoking brown imprint left on his shirt. "Don't worry, Warden. I'm sure they're not all dead. I know how you hate breaking your fatality record," Garr said before he stalked back through the people-littered floor to join the rest of his gang.

Danato had already thought of three or four plans to remedy his situation, but all of them involved being free and right now escaping his bondage would only lead to him being put down by the elementals. There was only one hope left.

He looked around the room for Belus, but didn't see him. That meant that he hadn't been captured, but it also meant he was one of the eighteen potentially dead or severely wounded.

Danato's hope was slipping away faster than he could replenish it.

B ELUS STUMBLED INTO THE office, dragging one immobile leg behind him. Cori couldn't see his face, but she had a clear view of the stunted, bloody leg from under the desk. He grunted to a stop at the filing cabinet and sat down on the floor. He yanked open the bottom drawer and pulled out a first-aid kit.

She could see the syringe he used to draw liquid from a small vial. He injected it into his leg and sat back to rest. His stomach rose and fell progressively deeper and slower.

"Belus," she whispered.

She wasn't sure she had said it loud enough, but his body tensed and froze. He couldn't see her behind the desk. He hadn't been around for her short flight into the wall, so he had no reason to look for her there.

"Cori?" he whispered back, just as quietly. She thought he might have been questioning his lucidness.

"Behind the desk," she said. He mobilized, crawling and sliding across the floor. He emerged from behind the desk. "Belus." Her voice pitched when she saw his face.

If she hadn't felt like tenderized meat, she would have hugged him. Instead, she reached out and squeezed his arm. "I'm so happy to see you. I was afraid everyone was dead or something."

He sidled up to her and started checking her injuries. "The *'or something'* leaves a little to be desired, but we're amongst the living. At least most of us." Belus touched the back of her head. His hand returned full of blood. *Her* blood.

"Danato?" she asked, feeling tears line her eyes at the thought of him being amongst the dead.

"Danato is still alive," he stated flatly. He pulled out the first-aid kit he had dragged along with him and dug out antiseptic.

"How bad is it?"

He pulled her head down and dumped the antiseptic on her scalp. She could feel the burn, but the pain was inconsequential to what she had already been through. "I'm going to stitch up the cut on your head."

"I hurt so much." She lifted her head to look at him.

"I'll give you a shot of morphine when I'm done." Belus opened a sterile needle, pulled her head down again, and started sewing her up.

"What happened? Who did this?" she asked, wincing as he pulled the first knot to affix the skin.

"The elementals are out," Belus said, as if that was all the explanation she should need to answer for the chaos around them.

"The top-floor prisoners?" she clarified.

"The very same." He snapped the remaining thread off and prepared her shot.

"Danato always said they were the worst." Cori coughed into her hand. A splatter of blood speckled her palm. She showed it to Belus.

His eyes flickered between her hand and her eyes. He shook his head and gave her the injection in the arm. "We'll deal with internal bleeding later. First, we need to lock all four of these brats back up."

"Four?" she questioned, incredulous. "That's it?"

"It only took one to crack that wall with your body, and one to frostbite my entire right leg," he scowled. "Yes, four is plenty."

"They were out when Ethan and I arrived that first night, weren't they?"

"Yes," he said, getting himself up off the floor. His leg was slightly more mobile than when he came in, but she could tell he was still going to have trouble walking on it.

"That was what all the fire and lightning was about."

"Yes, they..." Belus shook his head. "I don't have time to give you a history. I'm sorry. We just need to get to the armory. We have specialized guns for them."

"Okay." Cori could always depend on Belus to be business as usual. He never had much patience for questions. Without thinking, Cori got up. Her head swirled, and she fell right back down. "I'm so dizzy."

"Cori," Belus said slowly and earnestly. "I would love to be the hero and say, 'just stay here and rest, while I get the guns,' but I can't. I have one bad leg and frankly, you're faster and stronger than me on a good day. We need to do this together or this whole place will be blown to hell with everyone in it." She was about to ask a blanketed "what," but she resisted. "Lockdown was started over an hour ago; we have less than two hours to get it shut off."

"They'll bomb us to prevent them from escaping?"

"Yes, that's the agreement. They are that dangerous. The military doesn't take chances." He braced himself on the wall and offered her his hand. "Let's go."

Cori stood with his help. The quick upward tug he lent her made her wonder if he was being generous by saying she was stronger than he was. She rested on the wall for a good minute before she could give him any forward movement. To his credit, he remained quiet while she marshaled the strength to walk.

Belus was able to walk on his leg, but he had to drag it up from behind like a peg leg. Around corners, he had to reposition it manually to get it back in line with his body.

They couldn't go directly to the weapons storage because it would send them right past the gym. Instead, they took the long way by the docks and through the kitchen. Outside of the kitchen, they sneaked down a slim hallway that was lined on either side with storage closets. One particular door marked "Utility" required security clearance to access.

Belus entered a code and slipped into the closet. Cori stood watch. The far end of the hall terminated with an exit that would put them outside, but it would be barred due to the lockdown. That meant they were in a long, narrow trap if anyone happened to come upon them.

Belus handed her a massive gun. It looked like a chubby machine gun, except for the four colored buttons on the side. Yellow, red, blue, and orange. He weighed her down with five more, strapping them over her head and under either arm. He emerged with ten more precariously balanced on his back.

He explained the purpose of the buttons like an automated recording, except that there was no pause or rewind option. Yellow fired electricity to arc the electrical current of Efrat. The red was a fire burst to fend off Hirem and his icy attacks. The blue defended against Garr's fire. The orange dispersed Remi's water attacks

As if that wasn't enough, the gun came with a flashlight, laser aim, and was resistant to hot and cold. Just in case someone tried to burn it out of her hands, or freeze it to them. The technology was beyond anything she was aware of, but clearly her awareness had been nullified the second she met Danato.

Cori's hands were shaking. She wasn't sure if it was from shock or fear. Belus grabbed her by the elbow and pulled her forward. "This is a warden's job."

She wanted to tell him she wouldn't get that job. She wanted to tell him she was too scared, too hurt, and too *noncompliant* to do what he was asking of her, but he wasn't the type of person who would take "no" for an answer.

He was doing his job. He was saving the day. All she had to do was shut up and follow his lead. So she did.

After all, either she died storming the gym with him, or she died when they bombed the facility in two hours. It wasn't exactly the mental pep talk she wanted, but it would have to do for now.

As she followed Belus, she noticed how truly weak she was. Her legs were ready to fold. Her head hurt through the morphine he had given her. Aside from the cut on her scalp, she wasn't bleeding. She was, however, feeling a congestion in her lungs that she knew wasn't from mucus. If it hadn't been for Belus pushing her onward, she would have laid down and given up back in the office.

"They have everyone quarantined in the gym," Belus declared as they once again took the long way around to the gym. He wanted to avoid windows and get a better angle on the door. She had no objection, except for the part about the route being longer.

"Belus, what are we going to do? What's the plan?" She donned six weapons that she had never used in her life. She wondered what clever plan he had to make her a useful asset.

"The elementals are working together this time. We will have to go in guns blazing. Just shoot, roll, and shoot. Cut a man loose and give him a gun. It doesn't matter who, just get more guns against the elementals than they have power to fight off."

Cori nodded. He had given her the rough cut of his plan on the way to the weapons closet, but the long version hadn't sounded much different. She had hoped that he was planning a distraction so she could get the men free, but he fully intended for her to be a part of the guns blazing. She didn't feel right about it. "The elementals don't usually work together?" she asked.

"They usually have an every-man-for-himself kind of mentality."

They skirted the wall approaching the glass-windowed door that went into the gym. Belus peered in the window. Over his head, she could see the elementals were in a cluster away from the prisoners. She had never seen them before, but they weren't hard to pick out, being the only ones standing.

Cori angled to see the captives. She saw Danato tied up next to Mr. Nose. Her heart sank, and she felt sick. She was relieved to see him alive and unharmed, but any residual hopes that Danato would be her white knight were gone. Ethan wasn't there to save her, either. She had no rock.

She admired Belus's straightforward, duty-calls bravery, but his plan lacked the shrewdness that the situation demanded. He was acting on his instincts, something she was very familiar with. His instincts were telling him to run into the face of danger to save his men; her instincts were telling her to back off.

"Are you ready?" he asked, pointing to one of her guns.

She nodded and put the gun in her hand. She recited the button designations in her head.

She wasn't ready. Her mind was screaming *no*. She didn't want to go in there.

"You can do this." Belus gave her a rare taste of encouragement.

She *could* do this. She was just being a coward. She *had* to do this.

Belus opened the door and ran in as best his leg could hold. She half expected to hear a war cry from him, but he just started firing his weapon; fire first, then electricity.

Cori moved forward to the door that was lingering open behind him. She made a quick plan. Run straight to the men while Belus was still distracting them. Cut the restraints with the laser and pass off every last gun. Then she could go pass out in a corner.

She reached out her hand to hold the door open for her not-so-heroic stunt. The door continued to close and brushed her trembling hand out of its way. It clicked as the latch coupled with the jam.

She stared at the door that she couldn't will herself to pull back open. Her eyes watered.

Coward. Coward. Coward.

She clenched her teeth as she heard Belus yell from the gym. She stepped away from the door. Her tears clouded her vision too much to see what was happening inside. She heard a final yell that might have been her name, but it stopped short.

She ran from the door to the elevators. She slipped in and pushed all the buttons in case someone came out to find her and follow her. Inside the metal box, she sank to the floor and prayed that Belus had not just died because of her.

She had many times felt the shame of her actions, but nothing compared to this. She was a sad, pathetic soldier, who had just traded her only chance to defeat the elementals for two more hours of her own life.

Even through the bruises on her back and the throbbing in her head, she felt her sorrow demon feeding on her. His gluttony weighed on her like a bowling ball.

He's dead.

"Shut up!" she screamed aloud to him. "Don't you think I know that?"

She knew very well that Vince was dead. He wasn't here to save her. Danato couldn't save her. Belus tried to save her, but she had deserted him. Ethan was gone, too.

She wanted to be her own rock and save the day, but she knew it was impossible. One person could not save this prison. She needed help, and she had no one left. All the good guys were gone.

Perhaps she needed to start recruiting bad guys.

26

"CLEOS!" CORI STUMBLED DOWN the hallway of the basement dungeon. The vampires that lined the cages on her path to Cleos were more than happy to see her. Their salivating fangs, outstretched claws, and cage humping were more than her nerves could take. She pushed the red button on one of her guns and shot flames across the cells. The inmates squealed and shrank back into darkness.

She knew Danato wouldn't approve of such viciousness, but she couldn't help but feel slightly vindicated by doing it.

"It's been a while," Cleos said from out of sight in his cage. "I must not be as alluring as I was in my youth."

She walked up to his cage. A little limp had developed in her right leg, where a painful bruise on her hip was preventing her from keeping a steady stride. As she came into his view, she could see comprehension rise in his face. He was lying on his bed reading, but when he took in her injuries and overall ruffled appearance, he threw the book away and stepped to the front of the cage.

He shoved his hand through the bars. She glanced down at it, a little offended by the demand. "It's faster than explaining," he said.

Her hand was still shaking from everything that had happened. Given what she was about to ask of him, she didn't want there to be any confusion about where her trust was going to land. She took his hand fully in hers.

A moment later, his eyes flickered behind closed lids and he inhaled as if that chocolate cake he had had was extra sweet. She grimaced at the pleasure he was receiving from her until he pulled back his hand suddenly.

He leaned against the bars, tears streaming from his eyes. He was now visibly shaking. Remarkably, the tremble in her hand was gone. Even her head felt a little less like a drum solo.

"What did you just do?" she asked.

"Transfer. It won't last forever, but you needed a little break."

She looked him over and leaned into the bars. "Thank you, but why did you do that for me? Not exactly chocolate cake for you this time."

"Let's skip the analysis of my character today. We're limited on time, are we not?"

"Yes, less than two hours now. I need your help. I don't know how to fix this."

Cleos backed away. "I know that's why you came here, but I don't know how to fix it, either. I'm afraid I won't be of any help to you."

Her eyes lowered, and she sunk her head into the bars. "I know that you're supposed to be the bad guy. I know if I had read your file, I probably wouldn't be here. I also know that I really need some support right now. Please don't be the villain right now. Please be more than the criminal creatures in this prison."

"I am most certainly more than that," he defended.

"Talk to me then. Help me figure this out. Tell me I can do something."

He stepped back to her. "What beats fire, ice, water, and voltage?"

Cori shrugged. "Nothing. At least not all together. That's why the guns have four different settings." She looked down at her gun. "I know one prisoner who loves fire, and he wouldn't be affected by electricity."

"You really are willing to do that?" he asked with suspicion in his voice.

"The prison is going down in two hours. Tell me that the rules and regulations matter right now."

He looked her over. It was almost lustful, but his smile said otherwise. "You're going to be an addiction for me as well, I think."

"Who likes the water, other than the mermaids?" she asked, getting them back on track. "I'm not on good terms with most of the animal level."

"You are forgetting one very important fact," he said, joining the track. "They are prisoners. They have no reason to help you. Nor do I."

Her eyes widened. She waited for another comment, but he crossed his arms and didn't let anything resembling a smile trickle to his face. She narrowed her eyes. "You son of a bitch. I offer my mind to you..."

"That's a separate deal. Any time you want to skip our study sessions; you go right ahead."

"You just took my pain away! Don't tell me that we haven't established enough of a rapport to warrant my asking for your help."

"Rapport!" He was up against the bars with her. They faced off like prize fighters about to pummel each other. "You think what we have is friendship? If you even comprehended what I have of you, you wouldn't dare to suggest that. I have more of you than any friend, relative, or lover could even dream of having. I have your mind. Just because you refuse to acknowledge how dangerous I am doesn't mean you have to treat me like a caged dog. I am not willing to do your dirty work for scraps of... chocolate cake."

He pulled away and paced in his cell. Her anger slipped away as she tried to comprehend the accusation laid at her feet. She realized she had made a grave miscalculation in trusting him as blindly as she had, but at that point, he was all she had. She had no choice but to lie in her bed of ignorance and hope no one stabbed her in her slumber.

"I'm sorry, Cleos." His head whipped back to her with a hard stare, like she had just insulted him. "You're right. If you know me as well as you claim, then you know that I was considering bribing the other inmates with perks to get them to help me. So I shall offer you the same. What do you want?"

He moved to the bars, slamming his hands on them and shaking them. The door rattled slightly, but otherwise the bars didn't offer the exhibition he was likely hoping for. "You don't understand. I could have anything from you. I know you too well. I could manipulate you like putty."

Cori groaned, feeling the pain in her head coming back. She rubbed her temples, trying to find some relief. "Okay." She looked back at him. "You want me to be afraid of you? You want me to understand that you are dangerous." She threw up her hands. "Done. I now cower before you, you great, all-powerful mind sucker. I will be your slave." He glared at her sarcasm. "Now, Cleos, or should I call you 'Master'?" She winked at him, which only spurred a colder glare from him.

"What do you want to do with the last two hours—err—" She looked at her watch. "—hour and a half of our life together? I can let you out, but as you know, we are in lockdown, so good luck with escaping. How about me?" She waved her hand down her body. "Shall I disrobe?" He gave her body a cursory glance, but he didn't seem tempted by the offer. "You've already told me you know me better than any lover, so you should be the best lay I ever had, right?

"No, better yet, why don't I just make you promises that I can't keep, because you and I both know I will have to grovel to get any minor perks out of Danato. That is, of course, if I'm still alive. All bets are off if I am dead, you know."

Cleos's glare softened, and he backed away from the bars.

"So, what do you want?"

He paused. "I want to be moved to a different level. I want to be away from these loud, hideous, uncivilized creatures."

Cori scoffed. "That's it?"

He nodded.

"You freakin' baby." She pulled her all-purpose janitorial keys from her pocket and unlocked his door. "Why didn't you just ask? I would gladly fight to get you off this level, with or without the risk of death over our heads. I hate these creatures as much as you." She motioned for him to come out after swinging the door open.

"Really? You'll do that?"

"Like I said, Danato is the man to ask, but I'll—" She stopped mid-sentence and dropped her jaw in sarcastic awe. She leaned against the doorframe. Even though it hurt her hip, she wasn't willing to let her reprisal performance lose any ferocity. "Oh!" Her voice dripped with derision. "The mind master doesn't know that I would be willing to do that for him?"

He shifted uncomfortably, taking her reproof respectfully.

"I guess knowing my brain inside and out still doesn't make you any better at predicting my decisions than it does anyone else."

"I have your memories—"

"Memories don't determine my decisions. My past reflects a great deal about myself, and my present is no doubt a great predictor of my future actions, but..." She got in his face. "I am my own person. I make my own decisions. I don't doubt that you do know me better than anyone I've ever been close to, but you don't know me better than I do."

He looked her over again, in that not-quite-lustful way. "Yes, very addictive."

She rolled her eyes and walked out. "Come on, we're running out of time."

27

"YOU KNOW THIS ISN'T going to bode well for your career prospects," Cleos said.

Cori looked across the elevator at him. His eyes looked red and puffy. Even though the lighting was at half power, she could tell he was uncomfortable being out of his dark surroundings. "I'm not up for that job anymore. You should know that."

"Mmm." He tipped his brow. "I would have predicted otherwise."

"Didn't you get the memo on Mr. Nose?"

"Yes, didn't you get the memo on Danato's unwavering devotion to the daughter he never had?" He smirked.

"Danato is also devoted to his job."

"You're right." He turned away from her and waited for the doors to open. "I'm sure he'll choose to follow that corporate dickhead instead of fighting for you."

She lifted an eyebrow. "Someday you and I will have to have a chat about how I feel about enigmatic men. Someday, when I'm not holding six multitasking M-60s."

He glanced at the guns and nodded.

The doors opened to the seducer's level, and they located their first potential partner. Cori stopped before a glass enclosure, which was frosted on the outside. She motioned for Cleos to back up and used the flame from her gun to defrost the window a little. As the frost melted away, an old albino woman with long hair and bright red eyes was revealed. "Onna." Cori stepped forward.

The woman smiled. "What can I do for you, sweetheart?"

Cori glanced back at Cleos, who shrugged.

"Onna, I'm Cori—"

"I know, dear. I've seen you around." The woman brushed some frost off her gray jumpsuit. "You haven't probably seen me much." She gestured to the glass that was already beginning to fog up again.

"I don't have much time to explain, so I can only hope that you are genuine in your pleasant nature." Cori raised her weapon and turned to show off the other five guns hanging from her shoulders. "The prison has been taken over by the elementals. I have a plan..." She glanced at Cleos. "We have a plan to free the guards."

Cleos stepped forward to the glass. It was a small gesture, but it made her feel confident that he was actually with her and not just along to watch the carnage play out. "I have to get these guns to the guards. The guards are being held captive in the gym. One of the elementals has powers similar to yours. You would be resistant to it. Is there any way I can get you to help us? I'm not offering you freedom, but if I can try to make you more comfortable. Is there anything that would make your sentence more tolerable?"

The old woman thought for a moment. "A defroster on my window would be nice. It's just part of being me, but it would be nice to have a view."

"A defroster, that's it? Any specialty items, food, clothes?"

"Hot chocolate," she said promptly.

"They don't let you have hot chocolate?"

"They do. Around the holidays, but it's always cold," she said with a smile.

"I think that—"

Cleos grabbed Cori's arm and whispered in her ear. "To give her *hot* chocolate, they would have to bring it to her, still boiling; it's a safety issue for the guards."

Cori nodded. "I'll get you a defroster, and I will personally bring you at least one hot, hot, hot chocolate around the holidays. Can I let you out under that truce?"

"Certainly, dear." Onna smiled.

"Please put your hands in the pass-way," Cori instructed her.

The woman placed her hands in a small opening that was designed for passing food through. Cleos touched her, but pulled back like she had stung him. "Wow!"

"What? Is she trustworthy?" Cori asked, inspecting the smiling albino woman.

"Very much so. She doesn't lie, but never ever put her in a box," Cleos said.

"A box?" Cori looked over the confines of her cell, wondering if that counted as a box. "What does that mean?"

"Claustrophobia," Cleos clarified.

"Revenge, dear," Onna said without her friendly smile. "Revenge placed me in this cell. A far more comfortable surrounding than my previous containment, I assure you. I have no ill will for this prison. I won't harm you or your friends. I will do as you ask and return to my cell."

Cori looked at Cleos, who was struggling to warm his hands. He nodded to her. "Really, she's okay. Trustworthy, just very deserving of her sentence." Cori didn't like the sound of that, but she was already in too deep to get fussy about the crimes her partners had committed. She pulled out her all-purpose janitorial keys and unlocked the door to Onna's cell.

28

"I WANT THREE SQUARES a day. None of this feed in bulk once a day crap. I'm a cecaelia, not a damn fish!" The half-human, half-octopus female, going by the name Aaryn, sat on the edge of her wading pool, listing the many things she desired in order to participate in the rescue. Her body was almost entirely humanoid except for the movement of her appendages. Her body didn't so much sit or stand as sway, an undulation akin to residents of the ocean floor.

Fingers and toes were all intact, but with a little more stretch in them. Despite the reference to an octopus, she had only four limbs, each of which had obscure suction cups. She looked relatively normal until you got close. "I want my pool cleaned twice a week, and I want a fountain put in for movement. My gills *are* functional; I should have oxygen in my water." She gestured to the thin flaps on her neck, which Cori wouldn't have noticed if she hadn't pointed them out.

Despite the long list of "needs," they were all easy enough to attain, and didn't seem to violate anyone's safety. "Agreed," Cori said with confidence. She nodded at Cleos to do his thing. He touched her hand. He must have received some resistance from her suckers, because he tugged rather firmly to break contact. He gave her a nod of approval. She noted a look of annoyance in his eyes, but she didn't have time to ask what it was about. "Are you capable of being out of the water for long?" she asked Aaryn.

"Only about an hour; more if this water elemental refreshes me, less if the fire boy dehydrates me."

"Get one more swim in, then. The next pickup is a little warm."

29

"Why should I help you?" Rodan, the lava rock monster, grumbled in his cell, still stiff from his last spray of water.

"Because I can get you a cage outside during the winter," Cori said.

"Outside..." His rock brow crunched as it lifted. "...in the cold air?"

"You could broil in bliss, but stay just cold enough to be slowly mobile. We wouldn't have to use the water that hardens you."

"No more water? No more stiff joints?" he asked. Cori nodded with a smile. "I want a bigger cage," he added, as if he couldn't wait to see what else he might be able to get out of this deal.

"We would have plenty of room to build a bigger cage," she conceded.

The lava monster glowed as his joy super-heated him.

Cleos leaned in behind her to whisper in her ear. "Do I have to read him? He looks pretty scalding."

"No, he's easy to control if he gets out of hand," Cori whispered back.

30

ORI, CLEOS, ONNA, AND Aaryn waited around the dock for Rodan to arrive in the freight elevator. They had all come down in one group, but Rodan was too large for the regular elevators, and too hot to be accompanied. They had a little while to wait since the lift was intolerably slow, even slower than the main ones. Plus, she wasn't sure Rodan was able to work the controls. There were only a few buttons, but with big fingers and a head of rock, who knows how long it might take him?

With nothing to focus on, she felt the pain in her head come back. She leaned against the wall and took in a few deep breaths. She closed her eyes and let herself rest just for a second.

When she opened her eyes, she saw Cleos staring at her from the pillar he was leaning against. He looked concerned. She locked eyes with him, wondering if he could tell what she was thinking at that moment. *Ouch*, should have been easy enough to predict.

He moved over to her, not taking his eyes from her. He stopped in front of her and raised his hands to her face. She grabbed them and shook her head. "You don't have to do that."

He drew back slightly as if he were going to abide by her request, but came forward again. He placed his hands on her face, with hers still overlapping his. She felt a slight release of her pain. "It may not last long," he said as he drew back, his eyes still filled with unease for her harrowing condition, indefinite as it was.

"If I don't make it through this..." she said. His chin rose defiantly, but he didn't offer her any objection. "Would you make sure Ethan knows how I feel about him? I mean, *really* feel."

"He'll know when you finally get the courage to tell him yourself," he scolded her.

She smiled. "Yes, Master Cleos."

He smiled at the designation, but the amusement was short-lived and he was back to admonishing her. "Don't let them get in a hit on you." He paused. "Not one." She nodded, understanding the implications.

A garbled ding announced Rodan's arrival, and the doors to the oversized freight elevator at the far end of the docks opened. The rock beast stepped out, followed by a precipitous wave of heat that forced everyone to take a few steps back. Aaryn moved all the way back to the entrance to maintain her waning moisture.

Cori checked the clock on the wall. "We only have twenty-eight minutes to get this prison under control before we go down with the ship. I am depending on all of you." She looked over each of them to drive that point home, in case betrayal was running through anyone's mind. "I'll go in to bring their attention away from the hostages. I don't want any human shields. You can follow once they are grouped to fight me. Just... don't wait too long."

Cori pulled her hair back into a sloppy bun and prepared for an all-out cardio workout. "My advice is to go after your equal. Draw their attention to you. As soon as they are aware of your comparable skills, they will start attacking whoever is vulnerable to them. Whenever possible, help each other out, because they will be helping each other. Cleos will come in after the fight has begun to hand out the additional weapons to the guards." Cori eyed Cleos, searching for an acknowledgement.

"I'll be in," he said, giving her the reassurance she needed.

"What about the lightning man?" Onna asked. "No one here controls lightning."

"I'll concentrate on him," Cori said. "But I have no defense against any of these prisoners, including all of you, so try not to kill me in the crossfire."

"We shall serve you well." Onna nodded to her.

"Thank you." Cori nodded back. "As soon as the elementals are subdued, you need to surrender to the guards."

"Yeah, yeah," Aaryn hollered over to her. "Let's get this going; lava man is drying me out."

Cori stepped over to Cleos and handed him all the weapons except one. She caught his eye several times, but she didn't know if she could convey anything to him beyond her indescribable fear, so she just kept looking away.

"Corinthia." His voice wasn't gentle. She looked up at him and saw the severity in his eyes again. "You know that egotistical, noncompliant, belligerent side that Mr. Nose is so concerned about?"

"Yes."

"That's who we need right now. We don't need a war hero or a brave knight or a werewolf rock. We need you."

She gulped, feeling more emotion than he had probably intended to incite. She was glad at that moment that he knew her better than anyone, because she'd needed to hear that. She rolled her shoulders, trying to take back a little slack from her sorrow demon. "All right, people, let's go find out why these elementals are such a big freakin' deal."

CORI STEPPED THROUGH THE gym door with her gun hanging at her side. For a moment, no one looked at her. Her entrance must have been quieter than she thought. The grouping of guards by the dragon's bay doors looked beaten down. Most of them had probably resigned themselves to death.

Amongst them was Danato, who could never look beaten down, but part of him, she could tell, had lost hope. Belus was beside him. His leg looked like a mere scratch to the gash on his face. A tinge of guilt filtered through her bravado, but she pushed it aside for later.

In the far corner, away from everyone, was a collection of four people: the infamous elementals. Cleos had given her a quick rundown of the group so she knew who to shoot what at. Garr, the tall, skinny blond in black, was the fire elemental. He leaned against the wall, popping sparks with the snap of his fingers.

Efrat, the one who had caused all her injuries, was pacing slowly. His lean, muscular build wasn't clad in a prescribed prison jumpsuit either, but it was nothing as showy as Garr's. He wore a pair of stone-wash blue jeans and a t-shirt covered by a plaid button-up shirt. His only embellishment was a large silver belt buckle. If he hadn't been standing with the others, she may never have recognized him as a prisoner, let alone her enemy.

His face wasn't the porcelain beauty of Garr's. It was rugged and indisputably handsome. His fair-haired five o'clock shadow wasn't as noticeable as some men's. His stick-straight, sand-colored hair was a little long, resting just over the curve in his ears. It flared out a little, making it look feathered.

His pacing matched the worry in his face. Something about this entire situation was causing him great unrest. Cori wondered if that something was the knowledge of their imminent death.

Remi, the water elemental, was the only one sitting. Comfortably cross-legged on the floor, she looked to be meditating with her hands upturned on her knees. A tight pony contained her long black hair. Her creamy skin and narrow eyes made her look Asian, but the breadth of her face said otherwise.

Hirem, the ice elemental, was leaning on the wall not far from Garr. His powers were not dissimilar to Onna's, but physically, he was her polar opposite. He had bronzed dark skin and hair. He looked Indian, but Cori couldn't be sure. He was shorter than everyone, including Remi, but his muscles were thick. He had ripped the sleeves off his gray jumpsuit, most likely out of necessity rather than rebellion. Even in his casual state, she could see the tight bulge in his biceps that she knew would be twice that size if he were flexing.

It had only taken a few seconds to gather her necessary Intel. After that, she saw no reason to hide her presence.

"Sorry I'm late." The room awakened. Guards, Danato, Belus, and the elementals lifted their heads, opened their eyes, and turned to her. An unintentional smile spread across her face. "Looks like I'm more than fashionably late. I always did love a memorable entrance, though."

She could see Danato and Belus fervently shaking their heads. The anger in their expressions belied the fear in their eyes. It should have been a warning to her, but instead, it was the boost of confidence she needed. Cleos had said she needed to be noncompliant. As long as they were shaking their heads, she knew she was on the right track.

The elementals exchanged looks as she came in a little farther, meeting them only halfway. Efrat, the electrical elemental, eyed her inquisitively. She noted his bright blue eyes. She had expected them to be brown. "Didn't I kill you earlier?" he said without sarcasm as he approached her.

She didn't detect any distinct accent. She wondered if he was American. She hadn't really thought about the origins of the elementals before now. "Yes, as a matter of fact, you did, Efrat." She used his name so he would be aware she knew more about them than they knew about her. "I'm running on a nine-lives insurance plan, though. I've got three left."

His head tipped in examination of her. He wasn't amused, but he appeared to be fascinated by her. Unfortunately, it was the same fascination that a cat held for a mouse. "Good. Each of my friends can kill you once."

"Dibs on last," Remi said, joining Efrat. Remi, on closer inspection, wasn't as attractive as she had been at a distance, but that might have only been because she was sneering.

"So nice of you to offer, Remi," Cori said, noting the name again, "but I don't think I'll survive the first one. You may want to reconsider your turn."

Remi reared, prepared to fire—or rather, *water*. Cori toggled the button on her weapon to orange.

"Wait." Efrat put his hand up to stop her. She reluctantly lowered her hands. "I would like to finish her. I hate to leave unfinished business."

"Me too," Cori said. "Which is why I'm here to kick your ass."

Efrat laughed. It wasn't a maniacal laugh, like a comic book villain. It was honest amusement. Once again, she wondered where these elementals had come from and how they had come to be imprisoned here.

"You are a sheep, little woman, and I am the big bad wolf. I'll give you five seconds to join your shepherd and his flock, or I stop your heart." His face was sincere. He would indeed let her surrender, now unharmed. That meant he didn't know about the jets that were only twenty-two minutes from turning the building into cinder and ash.

"No sweetie, I'm not the sheep. I'm the hunter." She switched her gun to fire and blasted Remi and Efrat with flames. They both leaped to the ground, ducking her attack. Remi countered with her water as she scrambled to a safer distance.

Garr walked toward Cori, apparently tagged in by his experience with fire. He formed a ball of his own fire and threw it at her. She easily ducked the ball, which made her wonder if he was giving her a warning similar to Efrat. However, he continued to advance, forcing her back with multiple flame bursts as she dodged or stifled them with the oxygen-depleting clouds her gun provided.

Seeing no achievement in her defensive tactics other than singed eyebrows, she switched her gun to electricity. She shot at Garr, hoping the change in strategy would get him off her back, but Efrat was in range to deflect the charge. His unnatural blue tentacles of electricity met with her gold ones and disappeared into oblivion.

She turned her attention back to Garr, who had thrown a fresh bundle of inferno at her. She flattened to the ground, escaping the bulk of the skin-melting heat. Her clothes, however, caught fire. Before she could perform the appropriate, albeit painful, *stop, drop, and roll* technique, she felt water on her back.

Aaryn joined the battle and quelled the fire with a quick swipe of her moisture-rich hands.

Efrat turned his attack on the new arrival. Lightning trickled from his fingers. Cori sat up and aimed a deflecting bolt at him. This time, the two streams collided in a blinding flash that was to no one's advantage.

While everyone was blinking away stars, Cori noticed that Hirem had not joined the fight yet. He seemed annoyed with the new battle and was astutely observing everyone, but nothing had coaxed him to retaliate... yet.

She heard a rumble and crash behind her. She looked back to see Rodan crashing through the gym wall, creating his own door. His arrival was fortuitous, since Garr was creating another ball of fire. He threw the rolling pyre right at her, leaving her no space to duck.

Rodan's arms and head wrapped around her to protect her from the blaze. Her fear of being cooked wasn't alleviated in the interior of his shelled protection, but his molten joints clamped tight, shutting out the bulk of the heat. It was still the hottest sauna she had ever been in, but it wouldn't kill her.

When Rodan released her, she saw Hirem had finally joined the fight. He was using his ice to attack Aaryn, pummeling her with a frosty wave. She was at risk of freezing to the floor like a tongue to a flagpole in winter, but Onna turned his torrent of freezing snow into snowflakes that fell before they reached Aaryn.

Hirem looked at Onna, angry and surprised. She waved her fingers at him daintily. "I'm not a hack-job, dear," she said, answering whatever questions he had about her skillset.

Remi, in the meantime, had caught onto the game and went after Rodan to saturate his hot lava joints. Aaryn dove into the path of her water spray, soaking it up like a sponge. "Oh, thank you, I needed that," she quipped.

Garr threw more fireballs at Aaryn, but her refreshed flexibility became her defense. She shifted and bent in ways a yogi could only dream of. Even Hirem's ice barrages were useless since none of them could hit her.

Remi turned her water attack back to Rodan, but with a simple wave of her hand, Onna turned the water into icicles that shattered against Rodan's rock body.

Efrat, in an attempt to help his cohorts, shot out bolts every which way. Cori stopped each one with her dampening shot. He paused and looked her over again. His fascination with the puny insect before him was rapidly turning into impatience for the nuisance rodent he couldn't quite trap.

She smiled at him. She knew she shouldn't. She knew it would only egg him on, but she couldn't help but enjoy being the pain in his ass. As she suspected, her audacity baited him. He advanced on her, ignoring everyone in the room. Unfortunately, everyone in the room was too preoccupied to come to her rescue.

Cori backed away from him, leaving her farther from her comrades, but she didn't know what else to do. She knew it would only take one more attack to kill her. As it was, she wasn't feeling too good. Her head no longer hurt, but her eyes were getting blurry. That wasn't a good sign.

She countered two more of his bolts. He still advanced. The wall was gaining on her; diminishing the ground she could retreat to. She changed her attack. She switched settings and hit him with a spray of fog, temporarily depriving him of oxygen. It might have served well to extinguish a comrade on fire, but aside from a sudden fit of coughing and hand waving to clear the cloud, Efrat was unaffected. The lame attack did, however, stop his advance.

"Why did you do that?"

"I was getting bored with the back and forth. I thought I'd try something else." She frowned.

"So am I. That's why I'm going to bash your head into the wall... again."

Behind Efrat, Cori could see that Remi had redirected her attack back to Onna. Her water hit had frozen the old woman in place and she was struggling to release herself while defending further attacks.

Rodan spat a lava ball near her to melt her free.

Aaryn had sacrificed herself and jumped on Hirem to protect Onna in her vulnerable state. Hirem's super freezing hands and her super moist body had stuck together. Cori might have found it amusing if she hadn't had the image of the tongue on the flagpole still in her mind.

Cori deflected another bolt from Efrat. He wasn't so much advancing now as intimidating her. She knew the battle was turning and so did he. She got the impression from the delight in his eyes that he was indeed planning to finish her off.

Garr blasted Onna with a steady surge of fire. It seemed to take all her energy to create a shield of ice to keep her safe. With his ice protector occupied, Rodan was at the mercy of Remi, who was producing a deluge to immobilize him. Cori could hear the beast's joints crack as they turned rigid.

The unfolding scene forced Cori to lower her armament and resort to her tried-and-true defense: her mouth. It was a long shot, but there was one question that had slowly been forming in the back of her foggy mind.

Her surrender took Efrat by surprise. Once his astonishment passed, he stalked forward for a physical confrontation.

"Why haven't you killed me?" she asked.

He stopped. His eyes looked her over like she had asked him for a light in a burning building. "I'm working on that, *sweetie*," he retorted.

"No, you're not." She didn't really know what her point was, or if it mattered, but her mind was slowly forming an argument for her off-the-cuff verbal stall. "You gave me five seconds. You've been holding back your attacks. Even Garr threw a few attacks that were easy to duck. You all could have fired at once, but you didn't." His face revealed nothing for her to interpret. "You clearly have control, so why hostages instead of victims? You're the bad guy, right? Why aren't you killing everyone?"

His examination of her never stopped, but the smug smile faded momentarily. His eyes narrowed and his lips twitched slightly toward a frown. "Yeah, *I'm* the bad guy," he ground out. "I don't know what you think is going on here, sheep, but your interpretation is just as skewed as the rest of them." He raised hands that were trickling with veins of blue. "As far as I'm concerned, this is self-defense."

She must have looked crestfallen, because his smirk reappeared. She lost focus, finally giving in to the muzzle on her brain function. He raised his hands and fired. She didn't fire back. An electrical storm of blue and gold danced in front of her. She was so out of it, it took her several seconds to realize the glittering display was from the bolt being deflected.

The shots came from beside her. She turned and saw guards protecting her from Efrat's attack. A frontal assault was being waged against the other three elementals. The guards were even smart enough to free Rodan to help. Someone dumped water on Aaryn to free her from Hirem before they attacked him.

Cori surveyed the room and saw Danato ordering the guards and directing the attack. Belus was too wounded to do much, but he was helping free more guards. Cleos was collecting the stash of weapons they had taken off Belus and was handing them out as well. She caught sight of Mr. Nose, who was staring at her with stunned awe. She smiled at him and started laughing. Her disregard for the rules was saving that asshole's life.

She caught Danato's attention, and he grabbed the first guard to pass him and pointed her out to him. The guard's eyes widened, and he sprinted toward her, apparently eager to do Danato's bidding and fetch her. Her muddled brain couldn't begin to register the earnest concern on his face as he barreled toward her.

She turned back to the tapering battle and jumped at the sight of Efrat only inches away from her. His hands snapped with power, outstretched to strangle the last of her life away, but his attack had been stalled. The two guards currently preventing her demise had lassoed his shoulders to drag him back, but Efrat was still inching forward in slow motion, no doubt propelled by the sheer will of the murderous intent his angry blue eyes were broadcasting to her.

Without the energy to fight or flee, she stumbled back, flopping on the floor before his hands could grip her neck. The minion guard sent to help her arrived and used the force of his velocity to coldcock Efrat.

Cori heard the bone-on-bone smack as Efrat's head twisted to the side and he went limp. With wide eyes and a slight pant from his exertion, the guard turned to her and helped her off the floor. She stared at him with increasing awe for his one-punch knockout. He might have even broken Efrat's jaw. "Thanks-" she finally thought to say.

"My pleasure, ma'am." He braced her arm and walked her away from the battle scene. "It's the least I can do. You did save our butts, after all." He looked familiar and his southern drawl reminded her of the man who had saved her from being raped when she first came to the prison. If it was the same man, then this was the second debt of gratitude she owed him.

She gave up trying to decipher his identity since her brain was about to explode and concentrated on walking.

She was brought straight to Danato. He didn't look happy to see her. She didn't know what kind of trouble she was in, but she presumed that he would wait to yell at her in private. As he looked her over, his demeanor softened. Nothing about her wounds were obvious, but judging by how weak she felt, she could imagine how she looked.

She noticed Cleos shift behind Danato, his hands already freshly cuffed.

"Cleos." She moved away from the crutch of her guard to check on him, but Danato stepped in her way.

"Why is he out?" Danato asked.

Cori stepped back in shock. "You had a front-row seat, Danato; please don't tell me you missed the part where *we* saved the day."

"He is not to be trusted, Cori." Danato lowered his voice, despite the fact that Cleos was only a few feet away and could hear him just fine. "You need to stay away from him."

Cori slowly stepped around Danato. She kept eye contact with him as she did. She sidled up to Cleos and took his arm, partially for effect, but also because she was too dizzy to stand on her own. "I couldn't have done this without him. I won't let you—"

"Cori." Cleos spoke softly, but it was enough to stop her rant. "You should step away from me."

She searched his eyes for some explanation for this slight, but he was already pulling his arm from her grasp. "What?" she asked, appalled.

"Just a little space, please," he said.

Cori stepped away, staring at him with condemning shock. "What the hell is wrong with—?" Before she could finish, she convulsed and vomited up blood. She observed the blood splattered at her feet. She looked back at Cleos, who gave her a sympathetic *I told you so* smile. "Oh, right."

C ORI WOKE IN THE infirmary. It was her second
week in recovery. According to Danato, they'd had
to tap her skull to relieve the hemorrhaging pressure on
her brain. She had spent some time in surgery after that
so they could repair the internal damage that was leaking
blood into her lungs and stomach.

She later learned he had underplayed the seriousness of
the wounds. The nurses told the story a little differently.
Her blood pressure had plummeted so severely during the
emergency drain that they had to restart her heart. After
several transfusions, two resuscitations, and a boatload of
drugs, the names of which she couldn't pronounce, she
was alive and kicking.

Well, the kicking had yet to come, but she was alive.

And bored.

The boredom was more of a punishment than the
recovery pain. Danato visited with her every day. They
discussed her actions pleasantly, albeit with a few tense
moments. He was careful not to suggest that her actions

were wrong since they clearly saved the prison, but there was a lot of debate about the promises she had made to the inmates that helped her.

After some lengthy back and forth, he conceded to abide by whatever requests were reasonable and didn't require excessive paperwork to the board. Other than that, he refused to offer a timeline, nor would he promise that all the prisoners would receive a reward of some kind.

Cori had expected to see him again when she woke that morning, but an unfamiliar face waited for her. In the room's corner, a man sat against the wall, reading. His broad shoulders overshadowed the tiny plastic chair he was sitting in. His brawny frame made him look overweight, but on closer inspection, he was in rather good shape. His black slacks and black button-down shirt seemed to beg for a priest's collar, but the three unfastened buttons exhibiting his neck and chest said otherwise. He wore tiny oval-shaped spectacles that were just barely tinted.

His hair was dark auburn, with flyaway hairs that demanded to stand tall, whether or not he wanted them to. A slight smile lit his face as he sat reading. She wasn't sure if that was a permanent fixture to his face, or if his book was amusing him.

The book looked like one of the many red bound books Danato kept in his study, the books she couldn't get her brain around. "Are you another corporate guru?" she asked with a hoarse throat.

He looked up at her and his smile spread. It enhanced his features, which could otherwise have been described as plain. He placed a bookmark in his book and folded it shut. "No." He stood and approached her, removing his tinted spectacles.

His eyes were black.

Not the type of black that people used to describe the very darkest of brown eyes. They were black like the pupil had taken up the whole eye, leaving no room for the iris. He must have noticed her gawking at him, because he slipped his glasses back on.

He stopped at her bedside table and poured her a glass of water. "I'm a friend of Ethan's," he said with a thick Irish accent.

Cori took the glass and drank from it. She kept glancing at him as she drank. She had questions for him, but she had been forgetting to hydrate and the water was too refreshing to interrupt prematurely. "Ethan?" she verified after quenching her thirst.

"Yes." He took the glass from her and filled it again.

"Is he here?" Cori glanced around the room just in case Ethan had discovered a magic cloak of invisibility and had yet to reveal himself. It wasn't entirely out of the range of possibilities, but he didn't appear.

"No." He handed her the water and sat down beside her on the mattress without invitation. "I'm Daniel." He put out his hand for her to shake.

"I'm Cori." She shook his hand. His grip was firm, a little too tight. His hands felt rough, rough like Danato's. "Why are you here? Is Ethan okay?" she asked, suddenly remembering Danato's statistics on the longevity of hunters.

"Ethan's fine. He sent me to check on you." Daniel must have seen the question on her face, because he grinned and continued his explanation. "He heard about the jailbreak."

"Attempted jailbreak," she clarified proudly, and took another sip of her water.

"Ahh." He looked away from her, still holding his grin. He cleared his throat and seemed to get control of whatever amusement he was finding in the discussion. "He heard you were hurt... badly."

Cori shrugged. "Cracked ribs, internal bleeding, and a hole in my skull, but I don't know if *badly* describes it best." She left out the dying twice part.

"Just a bit banged up, then?" He pretended to fist her shoulder, but neglected to make any contact.

"Just a bit. Why didn't he come himself? Too busy?"

"He wanted to. I wouldn't let him."

Cori felt her mouth gape. Daniel said nothing. He held her gaze as evenly as she did his. "I am in bed recovering from the worst injuries I have received in my life, and you decided that my best friend shouldn't come to see me?"

"When he heard about the incident, he was beside himself with worry. I've never seen a man so impatient. He knew it would be days, maybe weeks, before he could hear how you were doing and he couldn't stand it. If it weren't for me and Heaton, he would have been here this morning, kneeling by your bedside."

Cori felt the rage she was containing bubble over. "What right did you have to stop him?" She leaned forward and cringed in pain. He gently pushed her back. "Get your hands off me," she seethed, containing her volume again.

"Easy, lass. I'm not here to make an enemy out of you. I'm here to protect my friend. He's a good friend and an excellent partner."

She wasn't sure Ethan needed protection from her, but she bit back her ire enough to find out why this man thought he did. "You work with him?"

"Yes, me and another fella. He's been a welcome addition to our team. He's doing well in his new job. He's caught more bounty in his first three months than I usually catch in six."

"He's a hard worker," she agreed. "He's enjoying himself, I hope."

"The job's hard, but he doesn't seem to mind it."

"What about outside of the job? Obviously, he's making new friends." Cori motioned to Daniel. "I suppose it's a bit of a boy's club in your line of work." She danced around the question; not wanting to outright ask. *Has he found someone else?*

"Oh, yes, work, pub, sleep, work, pub." Daniel laughed. "That lad does not hold his liquor well. You'd think he'd never had a drink in his life."

Cori nodded, wondering if Belus had ever snuck a drink with Ethan. "We don't get much alcohol under the warden's care."

"The first few times we went out to the pub, he would just complain nonstop about this girl he knew back here."

"Complain?" she asked.

"Oh, yeah, pain in the arse she was. One of those girls that likes you, but pretends she doesn't." Cori nodded, playing along with his passive aggressive game. "Apparently she's got issues. Baggage, you know? Like being hard to get wasn't enough. She's got trust issues, and intimacy issues."

"Intimacy issues?" She furrowed her brow. "Isn't that usually a man's issue?"

"Oh, sure, but when men aren't intimate, it means we're men; when women aren't intimate, it means they're hiding something."

"He said all this to you?" she asked.

"Not verbatim and not all at once. This is over many a Guinness. So, as near as we can tell, the girl likes him, but just won't bring herself to admit it because she thinks he isn't good enough for her."

"That's not…" She stopped herself from distracting her storyteller. Even if this game was leaving her personal life exposed, she wanted to know what Ethan had been saying about her to his new friends. "Ethan is a good man."

"Right, I know, but that was the theory. We're thinking Ethan's dodged a huge bullet. Like massive cannonball and chain, you know? But then something changed."

"What changed?" She tried to ask about it casually, but his pause left her sounding anxious.

"So, the first few weeks, the guy complains and bitches. The next few he's just quiet, kind of calm, like he's finally gotten the floozy out of his teeth, you know. Then he starts talking about her again.

"Now, my friend and I are groaning in our heads. 'Not this again.' But we be buds, so we listen. Not the same rant, though. He starts talking about how docile she is when you catch her off her game. He says she's the type of girl who has just enough book smarts to get her into trouble, and more than enough instincts to get her out of it.

"So, I was finally sick of hearing about the girl's blasted personality. I said, 'What's she look like?' Well, that was a mistake. He said, 'She's nothing special.'"

Her piqued interest fell with her face. She felt instantly sick. "Really?" she asked before lowering herself onto her bed. She didn't want to hear any more.

"As you might imagine, there was an uproar at the table. Why was this gobshite getting numb-brain over some girl that wasn't all that?

"He calms us down, and he explained. He said a woman views herself in only two ways. She's either something special, that is, she's gorgeous and hot, or she's nothing special, which means she isn't *that* gorgeous and she isn't *that* hot. He said the best kind of woman to have is the "nothing special" kind. Care to take a guess why?" He looked for a response from her.

"Because no man will try to steal her," she answered acerbically.

He laughed. "That's good. I like that. No, he said the something special girl already knows she's special. She doesn't need anything but to stay special, which, as any man knows, is a hard target to hit. With a nothing special girl, all you have to do is remind her that she's beautiful, remind her that she's hot. She'll never believe it, so you'll always be needed."

"So, Ethan wants an ugly girl, so she can need him to bolster her self-esteem?"

"No." Daniel shook his head. "He said he wants the pretty girl in the back row. He wants the girl that is going to appreciate him as much as he appreciates her."

She shifted uncomfortably in her bed. She no longer wanted to know what Ethan said about her in private. "So he's just pining then? What for? Clearly he isn't coming back for her."

A glimmer of amusement flickered in Daniel's eyes. He seemed to know she was just playing along to get information. "I wouldn't say pining. He's been out on a few dates." Cori looked up at him. She had no energy left to hide her jealousy. "That is what you wanted, isn't it?" he asked, ending the game of pretense. "You wanted him to get drunk and get laid."

Cori felt the full impact of her words coming back at her. She wiped away any hint of shame on her face. "I see why you came back instead of him." He tipped his head at her interpretation. "I'm the man-eater, and you've come to bid me to stay away from your friend, so I don't hurt him more than I already have." He smiled. She must have gotten it right. "I want whatever is best for Ethan. If I'm not good enough for him, then he can make that decision on his own. He doesn't need to send his lackey to threaten me, mob style."

"I think you underestimate how hard it was for him to leave you behind."

"I think you underestimate how hard it was for me to watch him leave," she ground out the words. "I respect your bond of friendship with him, but don't think for a second that your three months of beer guzzling overrides my connection to him. We came into this together. Every part of our new, weird, effed-up world is grounded in that bond. We are each other's normal. Distance isn't going to change that, and neither are you."

Daniel nodded. "I see."

"You should leave. If you would, please relay my condition to Ethan. He might be happy to know that I am not dead or dying. Unless you think it would be easier on him to think I am dead." She couldn't withhold the snappish remark.

He shook his head. "No, he will be overjoyed to hear you are recovering well. I will tell him you are full of piss and vinegar, as usual." He collected his book and headed to the door. "I'm sorry for upsetting you. I really did have Ethan's interests in mind."

She nodded. "I meant what I said. If you're Ethan's friend, then you won't have an enemy in me."

"Is there anything else you would like me to tell him, any words of affection or goodwill?"

She paused. "Yes, give him a list of my injuries: broken ribs, internal bleeding, and a hemorrhage in the brain. Tell him all that and then tell him none of it hurt as badly as him sending you here in his place."

33

CORI SPENT ANOTHER SIX days recovering before they let her leave the infirmary. Without work release though, she just wandered up and down the halls in a loose jogging outfit and shoes she may as well have stolen from an orthopedically challenged geriatric.

Her back still hurt and her legs felt weak, but she was moving, and that was all that mattered to her. She rounded the corner and slipped into Danato's office to see if he had anything she could do that wouldn't conflict with the doctor's orders.

Belus sat at his desk, signing paperwork. She had not seen him since the prison break. "Hey Belus. Is Danato around?" she asked as she slipped in the door.

He nodded and gathered up his papers. "He'll be back in a few minutes." "Good." Cori wobbled over to a chair and sat down with a controlled groan.

Belus clutched his documents and headed to the door.

"You don't have to leave. I'll just wait quietly if you need to work," she offered.

He looked back at her coldly. "I prefer to leave." He slammed the door behind him. The glass rattled, threatening to break, but it endured the abusive slam, just as it had many times before.

Cori stood again and followed him out the door. "Belus," she called after him. She followed him through the tight hallway away from Danato's office. She stopped short just inside the main foyer entrance when she felt a stitch snap under her bandages. She cursed.

Off to her right, Belus was on his way down the hall leading to the gym and kitchen. "Belus!" she yelled after him. He finally stopped and looked back at her. She limped toward him, holding her side just in case her insides tried to spill out. "Why are you...?" She looked into his scolding eyes. She forced herself to stand. "This is about the prison break."

Belus said nothing. She had never seen anger on his face; disgust and disapproval, but not anger. He wore it easier than she would have expected.

"You're mad—"

"Not mad. You saved us all," he announced with civility on his tongue, but not in his eyes.

She stopped her approach and kneeled down on one knee to bring her to eye level with him. It actually brought her beneath him, but it was appropriate either way. "That doesn't matter, though." She could read the resentment in his eyes. "I didn't follow your plan."

"Your plan worked." His words were almost congratulatory, but his face showed nothing but controlled fury.

"Yes, but..." Cori shook her head. "I didn't have your back." He said nothing. He was a proud man. Too proud to acknowledge any hurt feelings. "I get that. I know you think I'm just too stubborn to follow orders. Everyone thinks that. But that wasn't what stopped me. I didn't want to leave you. I hated doing that. I thought I was being weak, but that wasn't it. I just felt... I knew it was a futile fight."

"Clearly it was. You made the right choice."

"Stop giving me kudos. I know what you're thinking."

"Really? What am I thinking?" Belus asked, stepping closer to face her down with all his derision intact.

She fought back tears. She knew he wouldn't offer her any more sympathy with them. "You're thinking you could have respected me more for failing with you than succeeding on my own?"

His eyes flickered over hers. He nodded. "Something like that. I would have tried to fit the word 'deserter' in there somewhere." Belus pushed past her, despite her fragile state.

She grabbed the only clothing she could hold on to, which turned out to be his sleeve. He stopped short of dragging her on her belly. "Belus, I know you can hardly take me at my word, but I promise you, if I had felt right about the plan, I would have followed you into that room, even if that meant dying. I'm not a quitter, and I do have your back, just not when I know you're wrong."

"Isn't there a song about standing by your friends even though they're wrong?" he said.

"Yeah, a few, and they're all bullshit. A good friend should be the *first* to tell you that you're wrong. A good friend should have the fortitude to accept the criticism."

Belus pulled his sleeve away from her gruffly. "But you didn't tell me I was wrong, Cori. You just abandoned me." He walked away without looking back.

Cori wanted to yell at him. She wanted to grovel and beg for forgiveness, but Belus wouldn't respect her for that. He wasn't like Danato, who balanced his love and respect for her with his devotion to his job. Belus expected her to earn her rights every single time. Including the right to call him friend.

34

Cori's arrival in Danato's office surprised him. He rushed over to help her to a chair and shut the door behind her. "I thought you would be at home."

"I've been in bed for the last three weeks. I need something to do."

"Well, I sympathize, but I don't know what you can do." He sat down at his desk.

"I thought you would have been desperate to have me back."

He smiled. "I am. As soon as you're ready. Until then, you can study for your written test."

"You got me back in the running?"

"Yes, Mr. Godfrey was more than thrilled with your performance since you saved his butt. Not to mention I sent him a copy of your medical chart. I insisted that anyone capable of recovering the prison when they are that close to death deserves the right to complete the application process." Danato hated the sound of the word death in reference to her. He knew the job was a risk, and he knew Cori was up for the challenge, but part of him wished he hadn't let her apply.

Cori took a deep breath. "Just doing my part, boss." She said it jokingly, but he knew she was trying to be respectfully humble, like Ethan had always been with him.

He had noticed a change in her temperament toward him in the past months. She depended on Belus for her training and duty assignments. When she came to him, it was more for personal attention: conversation and advice. He knew it was partly because she missed Ethan, but he thought, or at least hoped, that she was relaxing her defenses with him.

"I wouldn't have been able to do it without Cleos. I know you disapprove of him, but he was better to me than the morphine was." Danato didn't want to hear her praises for the prisoner. "Where did you end up moving him to, anyway?"

"What do you mean?" He knew exactly what she meant.

"Have you built his dark room yet, or is he still in the basement?"

Danato didn't want to have this discussion this early in her healing. He didn't want to have this discussion at all, but he had no choice. He knew she would never let it go, and he had no intention of lying to her, lest he break that tenuous trust she had in him. "He is still in the basement."

"When will the room be finished?"

"It hasn't been started, and it won't be." Cori's icy glare left him wishing he had lied. "Aside from the obvious reasons not to," he explained, "there is no money for it, and the board would never approve the funds."

"I don't care about that. I made them a promise."

"A promise you could not back up." Danato shook his head.

"They saved us all," Cori argued.

"Yes, and they have been given as many incentives as we can provide without rewriting our rules to suit them."

"I'm sure that went over well with the lava monster."

"Actually," Danato chimed in, hoping to cheer her up. "Rodan has been moved outside. The thought process was sound. The water woman got pretty much everything she wanted too. I'm leaving the hot chocolate issue to you."

Cori's forehead crinkled in deep thought. "You're saying everyone got what they wanted except Cleos?" She pursed her lips with determination. "Danato—"

"Don't," Danato said flatly. He could see the wheels turning in her head. She was preparing a full-on debate to win the issue. It would be a pointless argument that would only end with him asserting his authority. "I've explored every option. There is no way to move him without violating prison standards."

"It's just one prisoner."

"I know your conviction, Cori, but understand that moving one prisoner is not just about space and cost. If I move him, I have to take into consideration the vulnerabilities of every prisoner around him and his to them. I can't move him if it will risk lives to do so."

"You don't trust him."

Danato didn't like the statement. It meant that she *did* trust him. He had, up to this point, resisted the urge to ban her from seeing him. He knew that would only put a match to her gasoline. "I don't trust any of the prisoners. I have already spoken with him. We've come to a few minor agreements which will make him more comfortable. He was moved to a bigger cell, and he has been given better furnishings."

Cori stood up and went to the door for her dramatic exit.

"Cori." He knew she wasn't giving up yet. She turned back. He resisted the urge to ask her to sit back down. "This discussion is over." He tried his best to soften his voice. "I've done what can be done. If you plan to take over this job, you will need to be prepared for disappointment."

"I assure you, I am," she said before giving the door its second round of abuse for the day.

35

E THAN RAN ACROSS GRAVELED roofs, giving chase to his prey. At the first alley, he skipped the vacancy with ease. However, the next gap was a good deal wider. With little hope of landing on the other side, he jumped.

For several seconds, his feet dangled in the air, searching for solid ground. When the last hope of reaching the next building left him, he gave in to the plummet with a long, drawn-out curse.

Two men on the roof behind him skidded to a halt at the roof's edge just in time to see him miss his target. "Ethan, you crazy son of a bitch!" they yelled from above as he fell.

Ethan's skin burned as the pool below slapped him harshly. He went under, hoping he had landed in the deep end. He hit the bottom with a nice bump and relaxed into the atmosphere of muted senses.

Overhead, he could hear his friends laughing and yelling. He waited several seconds before two splashes followed him into the pool. They swam to him to check if he was conscious. He crossed his arms under the water and shook his head, refusing to surface. They swam back up to wait for him on dry land.

After emerging and wringing out their clothes, Daniel, Ethan, and Heaton headed back to where they started. Heaton was a tall skinny black man who insisted on trying to pull off dreadlocks. So far, he was unsuccessful. He walked with a slight hitch in his step alongside Ethan, the last vestige of his shortened career in the British military.

They made their way back to an old Volkswagen van via sidewalk instead of roof.

"What were you thinking?" Daniel mused. "I mean, did you suddenly think, 'hey maybe I'll catch her this time.' I can't believe you even tried. Again!"

"Just because no one has ever caught one doesn't mean I can't try," Ethan defended his insanity.

"No, it just means you're stupid to try," Heaton chimed in as he opened the side door to make room on the back seat for wet coats to be draped.

"You knew there was a pool, right?" Daniel asked.

Ethan gave him an annoyed looked.

"Are you thick?" Daniel scolded. "You never would have made that jump in a million years; I hope to hell you knew there was a pool to catch you."

Ethan ripped off his coat and handed it to Heaton to hang up. "Haven't you ever tried to go beyond what the rules tell you?"

"The rules of gravity?"

"The werewolf rules!" Ethan shouted back.

Heaton and Daniel exchanged a look. Heaton put a finger to Ethan's chest. "They aren't rules. They are facts. The fact in this case is that no one has ever caught a female werewolf, therefore it is likely that no one ever will; therefore... un-catch-able."

Ethan glared at him as well. He still wasn't ready to believe that.

Heaton looked back at Daniel. "He still doesn't get it."

"I get it." Ethan shoved Heaton's finger away. "What's the harm in trying? It's sport, right: the most challenging hunt ever."

"Ethan." Daniel leaned sideways against the van. "The harm is: that werewolf was toying with you. She knew you couldn't jump that roof. She just basically double-dog dared you to jump it," Daniel pushed his hands off his temples, miming his brain being blown away, "and you did."

"Lucky for us," Heaton said. "She *did* know there was a pool there to catch you."

"The dangerous part is this," Daniel continued. "She has your scent. Any time she wants to mess with your head, she'll hunt you down. You'll conveniently find her, and think you have the drop on her, but she will already know your every move. Trust me, Ethan; Cori has got to be easier to catch than a fem-wolf."

"This isn't about that!" Ethan snapped.

"The hell you say. Freud would have a heyday. Of course, he would have thought you had an obsession with dogs, not Cori."

"It's nothing to do with her." Ethan ground his teeth.

"How did that go, anyway?" Heaton asked, walking around the van to the driver's side.

They all loaded into the vehicle with Heaton driving. Daniel settled into shotgun before he continued. "She's a lot more than he gave her credit for."

"Really?" Heaton glanced at Ethan in the seat behind Daniel.

"I said she was pretty," Ethan said from the back seat.

"Bullshit!" Daniel objected. "You made her out to be "Sarah, plain and tall." She's Cori, short and tight." Daniel gave a grunt and a hip thrust to add to his description. Ethan punched his shoulder.

"Doable?" Heaton asked.

"Totally." Daniel rubbed his shoulder. "If she weren't in such bad shape, I would have tried."

"You said she was fine. What's wrong with her?" Ethan asked.

Daniel glanced at Heaton. "I told you what was wrong. She is recovering well. I was referring to being in such bad shape over you. She was downright pissed when she realized you weren't going to be there."

"You didn't tell me that," Ethan said, trying to be only passively interested. He had poured his heart out numerous times when he was drinking with these two, but he didn't like offering them his life story sober. He wasn't entirely sure why he did it drunk.

"Actually," Daniel continued, "she may have been pissed 'cause I told her every bleedin' thing you ever told us about her."

"What?" Ethan sat up straight in the back seat. He couldn't remember all his drunken confessions, but he knew some of them were rather hostile in theme. "Like what?"

"That she wasn't that hot, but you'd do her anyway, because she's a safe investment."

Before Daniel could laugh at his exaggeration, Ethan's seat belt was off and he was around the seat with fists wrapped in Daniel's shirt, pushing it into his chin. "You son of a bitch, that's not what I said! She'll hate me now! How could you do that?"

Heaton stopped the van and grabbed Ethan's arm gently. "Ethan, he didn't say that to her. Daniel, tell him you didn't say that!"

Daniel sputtered under the pressure on his larynx. "I told her you appreciated a humble woman over a vain one."

Ethan loosened his grip. "You shouldn't have told her anything."

"I told her you thought about her all the time."

Ethan released his shirt. "Why did you speak to her at all? I just wanted to see if she was okay. Now she thinks I don't want to see her."

"She thinks you're resisting your feelings for her," Daniel said. "Which you are!"

Ethan sat back down and belted up. Heaton continued to drive.

"Why don't you just go back there?" Daniel ranted. "You want to be with her, so be with her."

"I'm not going to go back there to be with her, unless I can be *with* her. She has to make me an offer of love. She already knows how I feel. If I stay and we do nothing but bicker and dance around our feelings, what's the point? I don't need a woman to grant my every desire, but I at least want one that wants me around."

"I'm telling you, she does," Daniel exclaimed.

"If I walked into that prison tomorrow, would she smile and come rushing to greet me?" Ethan asked, knowing full well that nothing was ever that easily interpreted with Cori.

Daniel exchanged another look with Heaton.

"Will you stop doing that?" Ethan yelled. "Just tell me."

"Honestly," Daniel said, "I think she would still be a little offish to you, but only because her pride hasn't been hurt enough to warrant showing all her cards."

"What does that even mean?" Ethan asked.

"It means she's stubborn as a mule," Heaton added.

Daniel nodded.

"I know that! What do I do about it?"

"You can't push a mule," Heaton offered.

Ethan slammed his fist into the ceiling of the van.

"Easy on the wheels," Heaton begged.

"I've been not pushing for a long time. I'm sick of being patient."

"That's why I didn't want you to go see her," Daniel said. "If you went to see her, you would have thrown yourself at her. She might have accepted you. She might have been scared off. I don't know crap about you two together, but the two of you apart is hurting her. Just give it a little while longer."

"You want me to hurt her a little longer?"

"Yes, and then I want you to go back to her with a smile and just enough flirtation to get her thinking about you, but not enough to get her on the defensive."

"This sounds so conniving."

"If you love her like you claim, then you hunt her down like you did that fem-wolf. Only you don't jump off the building. She does." Daniel paused to collect his metaphor. "And you aren't you; you're the pool."

Ethan chuckled at him. "You want me to bait her with my manly wiles—"

"Do men have wiles?" Heaton asked.

"Shut up," Ethan continued. "You want me to bait her, force her to make the leap of faith, and then I catch her?" Ethan thought about that plan. He liked it. He just wasn't confident that she would make the leap. One way or another, he was taking a leap, too.

36

CORI SKIDDED TO A stop in front of a glass-fronted square cell. "Cleos? Cleos!" Cleos sat within the cell, reading under the glow of blue light.

Cori jumped around in front of the cell, continuing to yell, while he sat calmly within. She waved a piece of paper frantically before him. Finally, she gave up and slammed her fist on the glass.

He looked up. He furrowed his brow and came to a two-sided box built into the glass enclosure. He pressed the button. "Hello, Cori."

"I took my test today!" she said unnecessarily, speaking into the box on her side.

"Oh, yes, that little endeavor. I really thought you would have quit trying for that after Ethan left."

"Why?" she asked.

"Oh, never mind. I overthink things. I didn't think you were fully healed up," Cleos said.

"Actually, I feel really good. Non-existent prisons get the best health care. No, I took the written test today."

"How did it go? Clearly horrible."

"What?" She perched her hands on her sides.

Cleos smiled. "I take it you passed."

"I got a ninety-two." Cori flattened the paper against the glass.

Cleos examined the paper test with the big red 92 and smiled.

"I needed an eighty-six to pass, and they said only the best wardens have gotten into the ninetieth percentile. I told Danato, and he was surprised. Actually, insultingly surprised. I'm wondering if I didn't score higher than him; he seemed a little perturbed."

Cleos nodded, taking in her ranting, overlapping sentences.

"I just wanted to come down here and thank you because I wouldn't have begun to know what to study if it weren't for you. I know this cage isn't what I promised you, but I guess it will do, right?"

Cleos nodded. "It's alright. Better than I expected of Danato. When do you take your physical exam?"

"Three weeks. Apparently, the board only comes in the summer months, not that I blame them. I'm terrified, though. I don't really know what to do to prepare."

"Sleep, eat, and exercise."

"I don't suppose you have any words of advice?" she asked.

"None you'll listen to," Cleos said.

"What do you mean? I listen to you."

"Cori," Cleos stepped closer to the glass. "Do you remember why you started this journey?"

"I didn't want to be somebody who needed to be taken care of. I wanted to be my own rock. I... why are you asking me this?" She didn't understand why he wasn't jumping up and down with joy. Or at the very least, congratulating her.

"I have an insight into your mind. Parts that you don't even pay attention to. I'm not sure completing your test is what you want."

"Why...?" Cori shook her head, trying to formulate a question. "Danato worked so hard to get me this opportunity. How will it look if I quit? How could anyone take me seriously after I made such a big deal about getting this job? I didn't think I could do it, but I got the elementals back in their cages, even when the military couldn't. Cleos, I've earned this."

"Yes, you have. I don't know your long-term future for certain, but from what I see in you, you may want to ask yourself what the wardenship will give you. If you figure that out before you compete, you might be happier in the long run."

"Okay." She slid her paper achievement off the glass wall and headed out. "I'm going to go show this to someone who actually gives a crap."

"Cori!" Cleos pressed closer to the glass. She looked back. "Cut your hair!"

"Why?"

"It's an unwanted appendage when it comes to fighting dragons."

37

DANATO ABRUPTLY HALTED AS he passed the downstairs bathroom. The door was half open and Cori stood in front of the mirror with scissors to her neck. "What are you doing?"

He barged in, prepared to stop a suicide attempt. He saw the tentative cut she had made lying against her chin. Six inches or so of flaxen hair lay in the sink, threatening to clog the drain. Cori looked at him with teary eyes. "What are you doing?" he asked softly.

"Cleos said that hair and dragons don't mix."

Danato's head tilted back as he added that concern to his own list of worries about her upcoming test. He didn't like that Cori had spoken with Cleos, but he had a valid point. "Yes, I didn't think of that. Any excessive length will provide an opportunity for him to snag you."

"It's just hair," she said, losing a tear.

Danato nodded.

"It will grow back," she said.

Danato nodded again. He understood he wasn't the one that needed convincing.

"Then why does it feel like a hysterectomy?"

Danato chuckled and hugged her from behind. "Because you think your femininity is dependent on it." He pulled her hair away from her face, looking at her reflection. "It's not."

"You cut it." She shoved the scissors at him.

He flinched away from them. "How is that a good idea?"

"If it looks horrible, I will have someone to blame." Danato laughed and took the scissors. He didn't have any experience cutting hair, but he went at her golden locks with the precision of a surgeon, one little lock at a time.

38

CORI RAN THROUGH THE halls of the prison, trying to maintain some semblance of calm. After a quick corner that sent her sliding into the adjacent wall, she stopped running and caught her breath.

She combed back her short bob-cut hair with her fingers. She checked her shirt for anything resembling that morning's breakfast. She even checked the zipper on her pants. Passing by an observation window, she checked her teeth for—once again—anything resembling breakfast. This also prompted her to check her breath.

She strolled into the truck dock slightly out of breath and rubbing her shoulder. Several of the loading attendants lounged by the door. They glanced at her with knowing smiles. She checked her watch before smoothing down her hair again.

"Either you're early, or he's late," the oldest man said.

"Men," she scoffed, shrugging her shoulders. She was about to leave rather than be gawked at by the attendants, but she heard the semi-trailer pull in. She checked her watch again and waited casually against the back wall while the vehicle backed into position against the door.

The attendants opened the bay door, and a gust of cold air filled the room from the gaps around the truck. Before they could open the truck, the door rose. Ethan stood on the other side, looking tired and unshaven.

His tight black stocking cap and leather jacket were probably just as cliché as Vince's long black trench coat had been, but it didn't seem to stop her from admiring the view. She smiled at his calm command as he strutted across the dock.

She took a step away from the wall to greet him. She pulled her lips down into a simpler smile so she wasn't grinning like a clown when he first saw her. She tipped her chin for a casual nod when she thought she was in close enough view. He glanced at her and gave a return head nod, after which he walked right on by to the exit.

Cori's brow dipped and her mouth dropped. All hopes and fantasies of rushing into each other's arms faded away. She had officially become the casual head-nod friend. Not even the friendly "Hi" friend, just a nod.

If she were mature and reserved, she would have quietly taken her abuse. If she were a little less socially stunted by her experiences in life, she might have assumed that he simply hadn't recognized her in her new haircut. If she were being logical, she would have announced her presence.

Unfortunately, her last bit of social grace went out the window when she saw the wet mop by the doorway.

E THAN HEADED AWAY FROM the delivery dock. He planned to check in with Danato, but as soon as he could get away, he wanted to hunt down Cori and tell her how much he'd missed her.

With this one thought in his mind, he passed by a waiting attendant without so much as a "Hello." He headed to the nearest exit.

With visions of surprising Cori with flowers from her own greenhouse, he felt the painful whiplash of a heavy, wet mop hitting the back of his head. With mop tendrils noodle-whipping his face, he turned to see his attacker.

The attendant he had passed just seconds earlier was enraged, standing at the end of the hall. Who knew a lack of courtesy could cause such incivility?

C

CORI STOOD AT ONE end of the hall like an angry bull, just short of snorting and stamping. Ethan faced off on the other end, looking baffled by the assault.

"Hello?" Cori said, propping her hands on her hips.

Ethan's face melted into shock. "Cori?" He laughed. "Is that you?"

Cori dropped her hands along with her shoulders. "Yes, I guess you've already forgotten me."

"No." Ethan removed the mop and jogged back to her. "I didn't recognize you." He looked her over. "You cut your hair."

He reached to touch her hair, but she pulled away.

"I guess that shows how much you look at my face." She took a step back, crossing her arms.

"It *shows* how preoccupied I was when I got here," Ethan assured her. "You look good." He stepped closer to her.

"Not too good, though." Her voice turned solemn as she remembered her conversation with his friend Daniel.

"What?"

"Danato is waiting for you." She brushed past him.

"Oh, how I missed this," he said, following behind her.

A FTER A QUICK MEET and greet in the office, Danato, Ethan, and Cori headed back to the house for a meal of Danato's welcome-back chili.

"How many have you caught?" Danato asked as he added yet another dash of salt to his bowl of chili.

"Only a dozen so far. It's harder than I thought," Ethan said, sipping on his wine. He had already scarfed down his first bowl, and intended on having another, but he was enjoying the sit-down part of the meal so much he wanted to draw it out a little.

"Dangerous too." Danato grabbed for the salt again. Cori snagged it from his grasp and gave him a hard stare. He seemed a little put off, but he said nothing more about it.

"Don't start; things are just as dangerous here." Ethan shook his head, not bothering to ask about the salt. "What about things around here?" He glanced at Cori. She had been working on the same bowl of chili for a half hour, even after fetching Danato a second bowl. "I heard you passed your written test."

Cori looked up and nodded. She went back to her chili.

Danato leaned in to catch her eye, but she didn't look at him. He looked back at Ethan with a raised brow. "She did very well. Surprisingly well."

"Stop saying 'surprisingly'," Cori scolded Danato.

"Yes, I'm sorry, that sounds uncomplimentary. I was pleased to see she exceeded my expectations of her. How's that?"

Cori shrugged. "Better."

"I'm surprised she didn't mention it the minute you got off the truck. She was very eager to tell you." Cori stood and picked up Danato's half-empty bowl. "Or did you not want to brag about that particular accomplishment?" he asked her as she moved into the kitchen to top off the bowl, even though he hadn't finished the first second helping.

"I guess not," she said.

"How's Belus?" Ethan asked. "I heard he got pretty banged up too when the elementals got out."

"Yes, he did. Nothing more bruised than his ego, but that's just Belus. I was more than happy to have Cori save my prison."

Cori returned with his chili and pulled a yellow bottle from her back pocket. Ethan couldn't see the label, but it appeared to be a no-salt seasoning. She showed it to

Danato before setting it down on the table by his bowl. He smiled at it.

Cori grabbed her half-eaten bowl and turned to leave. Danato grabbed her hand before she left. She looked at him. He winked at her and squeezed her hand before releasing her to put her dish in the sink.

Ethan gave Danato a questioning one-eyebrow lift when he brought his attention back to the conversation. He felt like the odd man out. He wondered if Cori had felt that way after her time away.

"Cori," Danato explained as he seasoned his food, "has been taking good care of me."

Ethan couldn't help but smile. He caught Cori's eye as she started packing up the leftover chili. "I wasn't aware that the great and powerful Danato needed taking care of."

"Well, if she hadn't been in cahoots with my medical staff, she wouldn't have either." Cori didn't look up at him, but a half-cocked grin spread across her face as she put the lid on her Tupperware. "It's only fair, since she's the cause of my high blood pressure to begin with." Cori's grin widened as she put her leftovers in the fridge. "Where was I? Oh, yes, why didn't you tell Ethan about your test score the minute he got off the truck?"

Cori shrugged, grabbing a towel to wipe down the table with. "I would have, but he was *preoccupied*." She drawled the last word as she wiped her spot off.

Ethan glanced at Danato. "Yes, I was preoccupied with the joy of seeing my friend again, but sadly, I forgot what a pain in the ass she is." He sipped his wine.

Danato looked between them. "How's that?"

"I didn't recognize her," he explained.

"Oh." Danato sat back in his chair. "I see. Well, that is understandable."

"I was right in front of him," Cori argued to Danato.

"You've had long hair since I've known you. You look different, and no, that doesn't mean you don't look good."

"I don't really have expectations for you in that area, anyway, do I?"

Ethan glanced at Danato to see if he understood that. "What does that mean?"

"It means you told your friend Daniel that I'm a wallflower."

Ethan stood, nearly spilling his wine on the way up. Danato reached over and took his glass from his hand, leaving him free to point an accusing finger at her. "That conversation was grossly misinterpreted, and I wasn't happy that he even spoke with you, let alone repeated my drunken babblings to you. If you wish to discuss my opinions of your beauty, I would be happy to save time for that later, but let's get back to the anger that you're harboring for me for this afternoon. I didn't recognize you, and you didn't say or do anything to encourage that recognition."

"I did say hello."

Ethan scoffed. "After you were already raging mad!" Danato stood and placed his hand on Ethan's shoulder. He wasn't insistent with his pressure. It was just a reminder to him that Danato wouldn't allow their argument to reach physical violence. Ethan hated that Danato even thought he would hurt Cori, but on this particular occasion, he at least appreciated being reminded that Danato was still in the room with them. "You should have said my name! You should have waved! You shouldn't have just let me walk away!"

Ethan panted, feeling the conclusion of his long-winded argument come to a close. Cori stared back at him, looking a little blown away. He wasn't sure if she was thinking the same thing he was. His last comment could have easily referred to their last encounter before he left. He probably meant it that way, too.

Everyone stood around the table, taking in the awkwardness of his outburst. An embarrassing dessert, following an acrimonious main course.

Cori cleared her throat. "You're absolutely right," she said, slightly hoarse despite her precursory harrumph. "I should have spoken up." Cori reached over and picked up his dirty bowl. "You guys can keep talking. I'm going to start the dishes." She reached for the bottle of wine and poured a little more wine into each of their glasses.

"Thank you, sweetheart," Danato said and sat again.

She headed into the kitchen and started running water for the dishes. With her back to them, Ethan and Danato were free to *converse.*

Ethan sat back down and rolled his eyes at Danato before taking a sip of his wine. Danato motioned for Ethan to go to her.

He shrugged back at him. He pointed at Cori and twirled his finger next to his head. *Crazy.*

Danato shook his head. He pointed at himself, swirled his finger at the surrounding house, and vaguely pointed to the prison. He pressed on his shoulders. *She has a lot on her shoulders.*

Ethan motioned to her and zipped his lips shut. *She won't talk.* He displayed a final snotty head toss to finish.

Danato pointed at him, made an alligator hand movement, and pointed to Cori. *You talk to her.*

Ethan pointed to himself. He pointed at Cori. He made a strangling motion.

Judging by the scowl on his face, Danato didn't like that gesture one bit. Given their history, it was a bit brash.

Ethan waved his hand to erase the gesture. He motioned to her and pulled his hands to his chest. *She needs to come to me.*

Danato shook his head. He pointed at Ethan and then pressed his hand on his chest. He leaned in for a response and mouthed *Do you love her?*

He nodded. *Yes.*

Danato pointed to her, then him, then his heart.

Ethan shrugged in response to what he thought was a question of her love.

Danato shook his head. He pointed to himself, his head, her, his heart, and then Ethan. *I know she loves you.* He pointed to Ethan with one hand; he pointed to Cori with the other, and then he brought his hands together in the middle.

Ethan nodded. Danato waved him passage to her before getting up and heading to his bedroom.

Ethan gulped down the last of his wine, and Danato's, before taking the empty glasses to the sink. Cori scrubbed her dishes with her back to him.

He came up behind her slowly and placed the wineglasses on her dirty side. She jumped. He braced his hands on either side of the sink, encapsulating her in a touch-less embrace.

"Hi," he said softly behind her ear.

"Hi," she said. "I got this. Don't worry about it."

"You did well on your test?" he asked.

"Yup," she said as she washed the wine glasses.

"Smart girl." He moved his left hand to tuck a piece of her soft hair behind her ear. "You cut your hair for the test, didn't you?"

"Yup." She nodded, pushing the same piece of hair behind her ear.

"That's smart too," he said, putting his hand back on the sink. He moved just slightly forward, so it was no longer a touch-less embrace. He kissed the back of her head. He wanted to kiss her neck. He wanted to pull her head back and kiss her lips, but he didn't. He kissed the back of her head.

"I guess."

"I like your haircut." She said nothing. "Getting back to the conversation you had with Daniel..." Her hands slowed until they finally gave up washing completely. "You are smart, cocky, stubborn, argumentative, beautiful, a pain in my ass, and sexy as hell." She said nothing, but he felt her body tense. "Did you hear me?" She nodded. He butted heads with her. "What did I say?"

"You said I'm a stubborn pain in your ass."

"Yes, and what else did I say?"

"You said I'm not ugly."

"Say it," he growled in her ear.

"You said I'm beautiful... and sexy," she whispered.

"Damn straight you are. From here on out, you are not allowed in a room alone with Daniel, understand?"

"Gladly."

"Now turn around and give me a hug, you stubborn pain in my ass. Damn if I didn't miss you." Cori turned and tucked her hands under his arms. He enveloped her body and rested his head on hers. He closed his eyes and drank in the smell of her apple shampoo. He could tell he was squeezing a little too hard, but he didn't want her to pull away too soon.

Even as he pulled her closer, she latched on that much tighter to his back. He couldn't help but feel the heat in her body tempting the heat in his. He was painfully aware of how their last heartfelt embrace had ended. As much as he wanted to relive that tender electric kiss, he wanted to stick to the plan. Until Cori acknowledged her feelings to him, or at the very least instigated an electric kiss herself, he wouldn't do anything.

When he opened his eyes and prepared to disengage, he saw a dark gray blob hanging on her back. "Holy crap." The blob unfurled and hissed lazily at him. His rat-like features were far less frightening than the girth of his belly. "Cori." Ethan pulled back and looked at her.

"I know; he's huge." Her face was fraught with embarrassment.

"What have you been feeding him?" he asked, examining the dip in her shoulder. "Please tell me I'm not the cause for all that."

"Not exactly," she groaned.

"Come on." Ethan took her hand, led her into the living room, and sat her on the couch. He sat on the armrest and massaged the sunken shoulder. She hissed as his hands found the source of strain on her muscles. After a little more pressure, she relaxed into his grip. He had had so few opportunities to touch her body freely. He couldn't help but think about other ways he wanted to touch her. "What is making him so fat?"

"First it was you. Then there was the rejection of my application for warden. Then there were the elementals, then you again." She took in a deep breath and cracked her neck. She exhaled an appreciative sigh. "There. I think I needed that."

Ethan eased the pressure on his hands and came to a good stopping point. He didn't want to stop, but he needed to. He slipped down between her and the arm of the couch. He sat behind her, hoping she might lean back against him, which she did.

"Why didn't you come back to see me after the elemental escape?" She shifted so she could look back at him.

He debated what to tell her, but he decided he needed to be honest. "Fear. Fear that you would be the same, and I would be the same. I may not have a sorrow demon on my shoulder to prove it, but it hurt like hell leaving the first time. I didn't want to do it again."

"What about now? What happens when you leave this time?"

"I'm still afraid, but I couldn't miss this. I wanted to see you kick dragon ass."

"Maybe you wouldn't have to go again. Maybe you could just stay. You can be my Belus."

Ethan smiled. He reached for her hand, but stopped himself. "As much as I would like that, I'm kind of stuck. I've unfortunately paid the price for my loyalty. I have enough assignments to last me another six months. I don't exactly think I can quit and come back. Not unless that dragon gets the best of you tomorrow." Cori looked a little confused, but she nodded. "Oh, I almost forgot. I brought you something."

"What?"

"A gift."

A smile perked to her lips. "You got me a present?"

"Why don't you check my coat pocket?" He winked at her and nodded to the coat rack by the door.

She ran to the coat rack like a child to a Christmas tree and started digging through his pockets. He could have told her which pocket it was in, but he preferred to watch her scavenge. From his inside pocket she drew out a long blue hinged box, the type one finds necklaces in.

"Is this it?" He nodded. She walked back over and sat on the coffee table in front of him. Danato would have objected, but he wasn't there.

He repositioned himself to watch her open it, but she didn't. She stared at the box. "Aren't you going to open it?"

"I haven't gotten a present in..." She lost her smile, but only for a second. "Thank you."

"You're more thrilled with receiving the gift than the actual gift. Come on, you're making me antsy."

Cori bit her lower lip and opened the box. Nine brightly polished gold rings lined the box. Her smile faded and her shoulders dropped. She looked up at him.

He grimaced. "I'm sorry, Cori. I thought they would be right up your alley. You don't have to wear them."

"They're perfect," she said, regaining her smile.

"Are you sure? I had them made from that wizard's medallion necklace I... stole."

"Why only nine? Did they run out?" she asked.

"No, I have the tenth. I just didn't want to presume you wouldn't want to wear your original one." Ethan nodded at the old gold ring on her thumb. She took all nine gold rings from the box and placed them on her fingers. "I debated on size, but I can always get them fitted."

"They're perfect, Ethan. I can't believe you did this. I can't believe you thought of this, or even remembered..." She shook her head.

"So did I take a little snack away from that sorrow demon?"

She nodded. "You took a whole meal away." She paused, looking him over. "I really missed you."

"Well, of course. I'm the guy who brings you jewelry," he jibed.

"No," she said firmly. "I really missed you."

He nodded. It wasn't an admission of love by any means, but it was a step in the right direction. "That's good to hear, Cori. I really missed you, too."

"Can I show them to Danato?"

"Yeah, but don't tell him what they're made out of." Cori kissed him on the cheek and ran off to show Danato her nine little gifts.

40

As the morning went by, dignitaries arrived in groups of two and three. Cori greeted them all in the main foyer before the guards escorted each one to the gym. Danato introduced each of them as if she were royalty, and they, her loyal servants.

Transformed from a giant pseudo airplane hangar with a tiny little workout area, the gym was now a giant pseudo airplane hangar with a tiny little bleacher area. The hard, cold metal seating seemed inappropriate for the caliber of people arriving, but it was either that or stay standing.

Aside from a lack of snacks and beverages, the gym looked like a cocktail party. A low murmur of multiple languages spread over the room of fifty men and women.

Once everyone had arrived, Cori stood off to one side, looking the part of a wallflower. Only, instead of being shy and introverted with a preference for small intimate gatherings, she was terrified and asocial, with a preference for running like hell before the dragon arrived.

She wondered if everyone had come there purely out of bloodlust. She'd had only eight months to train for this test and there was a distinct possibility that she might die. Given the caliber of her competition, failure could mean being his lunch.

She looked around the room at all the smiling faces dressed in their Sunday best. They didn't seem concerned about the ensuing bloodbath of A-negative that would stain their designer clothes. Her Saturday worst—a pair of cargo pants and a "Bite Me" t-shirt—looked out of place. She had found great amusement in the t-shirt that morning, but as time went on, the humor waned.

"Don't," Danato said as he came to join her on the sidelines. He was also in his Sunday best, which turned out to be a good look for him: gray slacks and a matching button-up shirt with a black sweater vest. He was even clean-shaven, which was a rare concession.

She looked up at him, trying to find the source of his objection.

"Don't psych yourself out. These people have nothing to do with today."

"They are but mere observers to the untimely death of a stupid, stubborn girl," she quipped.

"I would normally object to the description of stupid," Danato said with a shrug, "but you are about to fight a dragon just so you can spend the remainder of your life trying to safeguard prisoners that at any moment could kill you."

Cori nodded. "I'm actually more concerned about the paperwork aspect," she deadpanned.

"As you should be," Danato retorted.

Cori waved to Ethan as he came in the door. She was relieved to see him in jeans and a t-shirt. Instead of his usual skintight black t-shirt, he wore a bright hot pink t-shirt with big words on the front that said, "*YES I AM.*" Cori smiled at the audacious shirt that already answered the question that it begged: "*You're wearing that?*" Suddenly, her own t-shirt didn't seem so out of place.

Danato gave Ethan a once over as he came in. Ethan grinned at him and propped his hands on his hips and nodded. "Was there something you wanted to ask me, Danato?" Ethan's head bobbed as if he were daring the big man to bite on the joke.

Danato shook his head and looked away, not willing to participate in the game. "You're as bad as she is." Ethan smirked over at her and she stretched her t-shirt out to show her style for the day. "Funny and slightly masochistic," he joked.

Cori smiled, pleased to offer someone amusement for her efforts, but she couldn't keep it long. She was feeling sick with nerves. This entire situation was a masochistic endeavor, and she was the star. A star that was about to fall.

"Belus," Ethan interrupted Belus's approach to Danato. "What do you think of my homage to Cori?"

Belus looked over the hot pink atrocity. A small smile played at the corner of his mouth. "I don't think that means what you think it does, kid." As Ethan re-examined his shirt, Belus turned to Danato. "They're ready."

"Okay." Danato nodded and glanced over at her. "Let's give it a few more minutes."

Belus nodded and moved back into the crowd.

Ethan looked over the bustling room. "What's with all the stiffs?"

"Observers, board members, and judges," Danato answered.

"Who are the judges?" Ethan said, pulling a granola bar from his pocket to snack on. Cori wondered if he always had one hidden on him.

"The three in the long gray robe-suits," Danato answered.

Ethan chuckled. "Oh, the *Star Trek* emissaries. Great, they look the part: reserved and condescending. I get why the board members would be here, but who are the observers? You're not selling tickets to this stuff, are you?"

"I suppose, in a roundabout way, we are. They're contributors. They pay the bills around here. Normally, we might only get thirty people, but I think the female element here has intrigued everyone."

"They can smell the carnage and they're here to watch," Cori mumbled. "Savages."

"Well, that's what I came for. How about you, Danato?" Ethan jabbed Danato.

"Don't tease her. She's nervous enough."

"She was joking. I was joking," Ethan defended.

"She wasn't joking."

Ethan eyed Cori from across Danato as if he might see this suggestive emotion dripping from her nose. "Cori, once that big fat beast comes at you, you won't even remember we're here."

Danato turned his head to Ethan. "Was that supposed to be encouragement?"

"She's going to do fine. She's fought this dragon over fifty times in the last few months. She's beaten her the last twelve times. She'll beat her again today. Test aced. Hurray for Cori." Ethan *raised the roof* but neglected the "*whoop-whoop*" that begged to accompany it.

Cori looked up at Danato, who returned her look of distress. "Ethan." Danato turned back to him. "Either you've forgotten, or I neglected to specify. Cori is fighting a male dragon today."

Ethan's cheerleading spark extinguished. He stared at Danato for a long moment, at the end of which he looked at her with a combination of apprehension and shame. He mumbled a sympathetic curse that, albeit sincere, lacked the inspiration of his previous statement.

Danato all but rolled his eyes at Ethan. "Listen, sweetheart..." He paused, looking her over. She waited for the inevitable: *You don't have to do this,* or *I'll be proud of you either way.* "We need to get started." Danato stalked off to announce the impending battle.

Her heart ached—she was having a heart attack.

Her stomach seized—she was going to puke.

Her head was spinning—she was going to pass out.

She wanted off this ride, but no one was going to let her off. Danato was her big strong teddy bear...well, *grizzly* bear protector. He wasn't offering any outs like she had expected. Then again, what could he do? Just announce to the board that he made a mistake in backing her? No, she had made her bed, and now she had to be eaten by a dragon.

Ethan stood just a few feet from her, still trying to comprehend what was about to happen.

"Any last words of advice?" she asked.

After a moment of thought, he shook his head. "I wish I knew what to tell you. I've never fought a male before."

Cori nodded. Advice or not, she knew the battle was hopeless. As much as she hated the idea of an unsurmountable challenge, she didn't really mind the thought of failing the test.

It had occurred to her last night that if she passed the test, she would become warden instead of Ethan. That four-months-too-late revelation made her realize that if

Ethan didn't become warden, he wouldn't come back to the prison. And if he didn't come back to the prison, what did it matter if she was the warden?

If she couldn't have Ethan, she didn't want any of it. Because he was the only thing that made this place tolerable, even fun.

So, there she was, knee deep in the shit that her ego shat. Her options were scarce. She couldn't just walk away. Danato was clearly not offering that. She couldn't just surrender. Her lack of performance would humiliate and discredit Danato. She definitely couldn't win, or she would lose Ethan. Her only real option was to fail at trying to win.

No matter how she looked at it, she had to fight this dragon... and lose.

"Screw that!" Ethan said abruptly beside her. "You are going to kick ass. I don't know how you're going to do it, but I do know you are amazing. Everyone else is about to find out too," he said firmly, refusing to allow any doubt into his statement.

Cori smiled. He must have been pondering the negatives in his mind for a while before he decided it wasn't helping her to do so. "Thank you." She was glad that he had faith in her, even if it was just her dumb luck that motivated it. She felt bad that she would have to dash his high hopes. Perhaps he would feel better after giving her a consolatory kiss after the match.

The happy hour around them died down and the audience eagerly took their seats on the bleachers. Danato gave a curt announcement about the rules for spectators. No yelling at the competitors, no throwing objects, and no crossing this line lest your head be cut off or bitten off by said competitors.

Cori stretched her body and did a little light jogging. She had done a pre-workout earlier, but it mostly involved praying and bashing her head into the floor as punishment for her arrogance.

She took in a few deep breaths. She cleared her mind and focused on her strategy. *Almost win.*

She could save face for Danato, defend her right to compete, and win back Ethan if she put up a good, but not too good, fight. She glanced at Ethan, who was giving her a nod.

Belus approached with her shield and sword. She glanced around to see where Danato was. He was by the front door, preparing to release the dragon. She had wanted him to bring her gear. She had wanted his caring eyes to offer her reassurance at this moment.

She kneeled down to Belus and presented her arm for the shield. She searched his eyes for anything resembling friendship. She'd had a tenuous relationship with him before the elemental issues. Post-elementals, she would be lucky to get a mumbled, "Good luck."

He lashed the shield to her arm tightly. It hurt, but she said nothing. He held out her sword, and she gripped it. He repositioned her hand. "Keep your fingers a little loose until you start to attack," he said. "Otherwise, your grip will wear out before the battle is done."

She nodded, appreciating any words from his mouth.

"This shield," he continued, "is your weapon, your only weapon." He thumped the metal. "Concentrate on this first and foremost. It keeps you alive."

She shook her head fervently, keeping her eyes locked on his. She drank in his words like air to her lungs.

"Your sword is only used when you have the advantage, otherwise forget it exists. The male is faster, smarter, and meaner. He will pull every dirty trick that the female one does, but he will do it three times faster. You fall; you get back up. You get hit; you regroup. The vulnerable spots are still the same: the roof of the mouth, the feet, and under the tail. Don't rush your mind. Rush your body, but let your mind decide where and when to attack. Your body is in defensive until your mind gives it permission to be offensive. Understand?"

"Yes." Cori's voice caught, and she was shaking, but she felt exhilarated instead of terrified. She had just received the Belus version of encouraging words. His no-nonsense breakdown of the impending battle had done her more good than a heartfelt hug or perfunctory pep talk. He wasn't trying to make her feel better. He was trying to keep her alive. "Thank you." She searched his eyes for something more, just in case he might offer something in the way of a nod or a wink.

"Watch out for the fire." Belus backed away, and Cori heard the hangar door crack. She looked over at Danato, who had pulled the lever on the wall already. No turning back now. The dragon had been released.

CORI CENTERED HERSELF IN the battle zone as the hangar door raised.

The dragon emerged.

With tremendous speed and a loud shriek, not unlike an eagle, the shimmering green beast darted at her. Unprepared for a running-of-the-bulls attack, she tucked and rolled out of the creature's way.

She jumped back up, just as Belus had advised. It was fortunate, since the creature turned and blew a billowing cloud of flames after her. She tucked behind her heat-resistant shield. It barely covered her body, and 'heat-resistant' was a joke, since her arm felt like she was leaning on a hot griddle.

The 'almost win' strategy was laughable to her now. With the dragon's speed, guile, and talent for combustion, she would be lucky to make it out of here with a pulse.

The dragon darted at her again.

She braced herself, prepared for another tuck and roll, but he stopped. She waited for an attack from the slithery beast, but none came. The creature's long neck swayed its head like a cobra.

Cori glanced at Belus on the sidelines. Danato had joined him. They both stood with arms crossed, watching her. Ethan was pacing the line trying to find a spot to stand, but finding something wrong with his view no matter where he stood.

Belus gave her a nearly indiscernible headshake. She wasn't sure what he was objecting to. Her looking at him? Her standing still?

She raised her shield and set her sword. She moved toward the dragon for an offensive move. She hadn't thought beyond that, and it was probably why Belus had shaken his head at her. She was rushing the battle. She was letting the stillness of the beast instigate her attack. Her body shouldn't move unless she saw a weakness.

The dragon's snout struck her shield like a pecking chicken. The male was much smaller than the female, but his long, lean neck had enough strength to flatten her to the ground with one tap.

She didn't have time to get up. She ducked behind her shield, smelling a waft of petroleum even before feeling the heat penetrate her arm. As soon as the assault stopped, she rolled to one side and jumped up to defend her position.

Her position proved negotiable, though. Her feet went over her head. A sharp pain rose from somewhere on her legs, forcing a scream from her. She didn't know what had even tripped her. Only after did she see his tail sliding away.

She rolled and regrouped away from the dragon. She saw blood trailing after her. She looked at her legs and found two long gashes across her calves. He had slashed her with the horny ridges on his tail.

The dragon stalked her, not letting her recover. He darted and paused, only giving her enough time to get back up so he could make her move again. She was wearing out faster than she had planned. Almost winning was no longer on Cori's mind. Almost dying was.

Cori's sword ricocheted off the dragon's attacking claws. It batted at her like a plaything. Like a cat pawing at a mouse, first left, then right, all the while sitting calmly on its haunches.

To win the battle, she had to stab the dragon in one of three non-lethal but painful spots. Her usual attack spot was the roof of the mouth. Unfortunately, the dragon's fire-breathing capability had put that option on the back burner.

The next was between the toe pads of the feet. That gave her four targets, if she could make it past the claws.

The third was the underside of the tail, right where it meets the butt. Outside of the dragon deciding to take a bathroom break in the middle of the match, this was an unlikely option.

To lose the battle, she had to run out the clock, become mortally wounded and/or incapacitated, or surrender.

To surrender, she had to throw her shield and sword outside the gaming area. The dragon wouldn't attack once she gave this signal. Unfortunately, no one would believe she had tried to win if she surrendered this early. She had already established her tenacity, and now it was biting her in the ass. Not to mention that in order to raise empty hands, she would have to get the shield off her arm, which, thanks to Belus, was on tighter than a straightjacket.

She was hoping to avoid the latter two and run out the clock, but the longer she stayed in the fight, the more she risked taking door number two to the mortally wounded or incapacitated exit.

The beast blew another fire attack, but this time there wasn't a gaseous plume. The flames came out as raining fire. It was still on fire, but not nearly as pervasive. She wondered if he intended this or if it was a glitch in his throat.

She took the opening. With her shield as an umbrella, she ducked under the dragon's head and stabbed his shoulder. Her retreat was too slow. He countered with his paw. She flew through the air with the greatest of ease, just like the man... who got back-handed by an eight-ton dragon.

As if it didn't hurt enough to have a dragon bitch-slap your whole body, she landed with a jaw-rattling thump.

She allowed for a slight groan before willing herself up again.

She hurdled his swinging tail. On the leap over, she slashed it. Her blade only clinked off the ridges, but she was glad to get another parry in.

After another round of fire, Cori went in for a full-blown attack. She hoped to get to him just before he could blow another flame. Her initial run and war cry showed promise, but the dragon found her no threat at all.

Once she was within his reach, his head bowed. She didn't stop. As soon as he opened to breathe fire, she would stab his mouth. His mouth never opened. His snout drove her to the floor with another swift peck. His front paw pressed into her torso. His claws squeezed down on her shoulders.

He had just removed breathing from her list of autonomic nerve functions.

ETHAN MOVED FORWARD UNCONTROLLABLY when he saw Cori was pinned. Belus's hand shot out to block his forward movement. Ethan looked down at the red line he had almost crossed. Crossing it meant invalidating the test. He stepped back and came up on the other side of Danato. "What is he doing?"

Danato stood with his arms crossed, seemingly unfazed by the danger before them. "He's suffocating her," he stated, as if it was an everyday occurrence.

"I thought the dragons were trained not to kill."

Danato scoffed. "Try training a male dragon."

"Will he kill her?" Ethan had been shocked to discover Cori was fighting a male dragon. He knew she would not walk away unharmed, but the prospect of her actually dying was too much. He couldn't and wouldn't let that happen.

"If she doesn't toss that shield and sword off soon enough, he will."

"And you're okay with that?"

Danato turned and gave him a grave look. "She knew what she was getting into."

"She..." He stared blankly at the man, who was always first in line to protect Cori. Danato stood there, stern and silent, watching the fight like the rest of the spectators. Ethan paced back and forth, waiting for a reason to jump into the ring.

"If you enter the ring, her test will be voided," Danato reminded him.

"I know. Maybe that's for the best."

"What's that supposed to mean?" Danato asked.

Ethan shook his head and ran his fingers through his hair. "That should be me in there, not her."

"As I recall, you left us to go hunting."

Cori somehow freed herself from the dragon's grasp, and the fight continued. Ethan took in a breath he hadn't realized he needed.

Danato smiled, not taking his eyes off Cori.

"How can you stand there so calm?" Ethan seethed. "You act like she's nothing to you."

Danato's smile faded, and he turned to him. Anger ebbed in and then out of his eyes. "She is everything to me. As for my demeanor, it's not calm, it is restrained. I am restrained because I have faith in her."

"You think she'll survive this?"

Danato looked him over as if he was a foreign object to him. "I think she'll win this. Cori knew what she was up against today, and so did I. You don't see me quaking in my boots, because I know she'll win."

It was Ethan's turn to stare at the foreign object before him. Surely Danato was just being hopeful. He couldn't possibly think she would win. Ethan knew how clever and determined Cori was, but this was an insane trial to bear. No amount of dumb luck was going to beat a dragon.

"You're okay with that, aren't you?" Danato asked.

"What?"

"If she wins, you are okay with not being my successor?" Ethan didn't answer. "Are you okay with being a bounty hunter out there while Cori is my apprentice in here?" Ethan still didn't answer. He just turned back to watch the battle. His anxiety about Cori losing had waned. It was replaced with his angst about Cori winning. His chance to be warden was slipping away, right along with his chance to be with Cori.

C ORI NICKED THE DRAGON between the toes with her sword, and he released. She jumped up, feeling the familiar pain of broken ribs. Door number two was inching closer. She dodged several head pecks and claw slashes. She gripped her sword tight and swung blindly at the creature's snarling mouth.

She knew she shouldn't flail around. It was only going to tire her out and do nothing to win the fight. However, she couldn't resist at least getting a few swings in before she surrendered.

After a hard strike, she heard a *clink* followed by a scraping sound. She peeked around her shield and saw her sword tip skidding across the floor, followed by the tip of the dragon's tooth.

"Crap." She looked at her impotent sword. The flat edge would do nothing to penetrate the dragon's skin.

The dragon roared, his eagle screech now sounding more like a deep throat squawk. The result of her floundering attack displeased him, too.

The dragon bit down on her shield, bending it around her forearm. She stabbed at him with her sword, which was now a colossal butter knife. Desperate to get the beast to unclasp his hold on her, she jabbed the dull blade into his flaring nostril. She succeeded in her purpose. The creature released his bite. Unfortunately, he reared up fast enough to pull the sword with him.

With one perturbed snort, the dragon propelled the weapon outside the boundary lines. Cori watched it go. She looked at her shield, which was now a metal taco. She looked back at the judges. She was hoping they would call the match a tie and let her walk away consciously. The judges tapped their wrists. The time was finally running out.

She looked at the dragon. He was swaying back and forth, plotting his attack. She had no weapon and no defense. The beast wouldn't sit patiently while the last two minutes counted down on the clock.

She looked at Danato and Belus on the sidelines. They were both stoic.

She looked at Ethan. His eyes were big, and he was visibly anxious. He looked seconds from jumping in to save her.

She had to take door number three, after all. She had so wanted to walk away with a stalemate, but instead she would have to throw her shield outside the boundary and surrender. As much as it pained her ego, she was pleased to have made it this far. She had the right to be in that room, and no one could say otherwise.

She looked at Belus. She gave him a shrug. He gave her a nod. Permission. She had done her best. Now it was time to walk away. Maybe not with her pride intact, but at least her head.

She gripped the flattened metal shield and tugged on it. She was still lashed to the thing on top of being encased by it. She eyed the dragon, that was still swaying. He seemed to understand that she was attempting to surrender. She braced the edge on her thigh and tried to push it off. She hissed, feeling the sharp end where the metal had bent into a strict angle. It cut her thigh, adding to the tracks of blood that were dripping from her calves.

The dragon purred. At least that's what it sounded like. She looked up at him. The understanding he had held for her impending surrender was gone. He now seemed agitated. He didn't seem to like how long her surrender was taking.

"Shit," she slurred, taking a few steps back. That was a mistake.

The dragon spotted the subtle move and lunged. It didn't matter that the movement was backwards; it was movement. The game was on again, as far as he was concerned.

She leaped out of his way. Little had changed between this moment and the last. She was still injured. She was still tired. However, she was now renewed by her fear of death.

She had no sword to attack with. She had no shield to block the fire. She couldn't remove the damned thing to throw it away. She still had a minute left on the clock. She was already knocking on door number two.

She ran and slid around the back of the dragon. It was dangerous, but his fire was her biggest concern. She would rather be pummeled than burned.

She tripped over the whipping tail and landed on her back. The dragon turned to get her back in his sights.

She felt pressure release on her arm. It wasn't much, but maybe just enough to get it off. She tugged on the shield. It moved two inches and caught on something. By the searing pain in her forearm, she guessed it was caught on her skin.

The dragon screeched again. What he had found so offensive this time, she couldn't have guessed, but his mouth parted.

She could smell the petroleum on his breath.

She put her feet up on the shield and pushed. She felt the metal give, along with the pain of it scraping down her arm as it did.

She gripped the freed shield tight and jumped up. His head tipped back and his mouth opened wide. Surrendering her shield at this point was useless. The dragon wouldn't see her part with it and she would be Kentucky fried before he could comprehend she was weaponless.

Her best chance was to huddle behind the half shield, take door number two, and hope that she could survive her injuries.

In the hollow of his palate, Cori could see the reflected glow of the orange ember that was igniting in his throat. She looked down at the shield and changed her mind. She decided on a different tactic: misdirection.

She crouched, swinging the shield back and forward. She released it, hurling it toward the dragon's mouth. Even as she let it go, she ran away. She only needed a few more seconds to avoid his flame-throwing breath.

The taco shield hurtled into the dragon's mouth. With the sound of a shovel hitting dirt, it stuck in the dragon's palate. Out of the corner of her eye, as she passed, she saw the flicker of fire lap up into the dragon's mouth and fall back. The throat darkened as the ember within extinguished.

The dragon froze. Cori stopped behind him and waited for him to retaliate.

His head turned. She put her hands up and waved them. She even turned slightly to show off her back. She still had twenty seconds left on the clock. He had to acknowledge her surrender this time, or she was dead.

The dragon let out a sorrowful moan. His eyes clenched shut, and he lay down submissively on the floor. Cori's face softened as the creature continued to moan in agony about the shield taco poking him in the roof of his mouth.

The audience cheered and swarmed around her. The torrent of congratulations seemed out of place to her. She didn't entirely grasp what she had done. The *Star Trek* emissary judges surrounded her and read a prepared document that no doubt was a beautiful inauguration, but Cori couldn't hear most of it.

Despite her bruised ribs, random people were slapping her back, chucking her shoulder, and a few women even hugged her. She must have unwittingly just nominated herself as the new poster child for feminists everywhere.

She looked between heads at the sidelines. Belus was giving her a two-fisted cheer, like his favorite sports team had just won a big, fat, ugly trophy. She had never seen so much enthusiasm from him.

Danato was beaming at her. His smile was ear to ear. She was too far away to tell, but it almost seemed like his eyes were tearing up. Pride looked as good on him as his black sweater vest.

On the other side of Danato was Ethan. He didn't exude the same joy as everyone in the room. He was smiling, but his eyes told her his lips were lying. The smile on her face settled into a frown.

She realized what she had done. The shield had stuck in the roof of the dragon's mouth. That was all it took. It didn't matter that it wasn't her sword.

She had won.

Cori lost sight of everyone and everything around her. She was the new successor. Ethan didn't need to come back. She was all alone with her victory.

Cori felt sick again. The day's events were already too much, but the people crowding around her made her feel claustrophobic. The emotions clogged in her throat, making it hard to swallow, were adding to her smothered feeling.

She wanted out. She wanted away. She wanted no part of her brilliant triumph.

E THAN WATCHED AS CORI'S dumbfounded smile shrank away. Her face cringed and her cheeks filled with tears. She pushed through the crowd gruffly and ran out of the gym.

Ethan looked at Danato. "What just happened there? Is she alright?"

"Of course she's alright, she just won the prize. Couldn't you see how happy she was?"

Ethan's brow furrowed as he tried to comprehend what level of sarcasm Danato was on. "What is your game here?"

"This is what she wanted: to win. This is what you wanted: for her to take over your job, so you could go hunt. Can't you feel how happy you both are, Ethan?"

"I'm not happy. She's not happy."

"I don't understand." Danato's sarcasm melded with anger. "You want something different from this outcome?" Ethan frantically searched for the answer. "I'm sorry, I can't hear you. What do you want, Ethan? Speak!"

"I want her!" Ethan blurted out.

"And she wants you. If one of you would damn well say it, we could at least move on to the next issue."

Ethan looked Danato up and down. "Where were you yesterday, Captain Late? She already tested. She won. We can't be together now."

"First of all, I refuse to babysit both of you in your emotional chess match. Figure it out for yourselves. Second, I wasn't going to do anything to stop her from competing with that dragon, because that..." Danato pointed at the downed dragon, "...was beautiful. And third, who said you couldn't compete against her? Until you left to go hunt, you were both going to compete, anyway."

Ethan's mouth dropped. "I can still fight the dragon. If I beat the dragon in less time, I can take her spot."

"Yes."

"You'll let me come back?"

Danato's irritation faded away. "You were always my first choice. Now go, talk to Cori."

45

C ORI FOUND HER WAY to the part-time level and stood before the cage of her former lover. It was empty now. There were no remnants of him in the cell or in her life. He had been a brief, albeit important, part of it, but he was gone.

"Cori?"

She turned and saw Ethan standing not far from her. He had crept up so quietly she hadn't even heard him. She wondered if he had acquired that skill while bounty hunting, or if he had always been so light-footed.

Her eyes stung from her tears, but she couldn't stop them. She didn't hide them. She didn't even wipe her nose, which she knew was starting to run. There was no happy ending to primp for. "I'm so stupid."

He shifted slightly, placing his hands behind his back. He was ready to listen.

"When I came back, you were different. I was still the same, though. I didn't have enough time to catch up. I was angry, and hurt, and bitter. By the time I realized that you were the one person who could help me, love me, and tolerate me... That bitch Sophie was here." Cori tossed her head back, cringing away more emotion than she could speak through.

With a sniffle and a harrumph, she continued. "When I walked in on you with her. I felt... you know what I felt. But when you asked me if you should take the job, it wasn't because you needed to know what the right decision was. It was because you didn't want to feel guilty for making that decision. So I told you what you needed to hear.

"I told you to get drunk, and get laid, and you did just as I asked. It never occurred to me that I would be just as miserable without you here as you were without me. Last night... I should have just told you then. I should have just quit the test and let you take it instead.

"The only thing that stopped me was Danato. He had worked so hard to get me permission to compete. I came in today with the intention of losing. I figured if I lost, you would have to take the test. You would win, and then you would have to come back." Her shoulder ached. She rolled it and rubbed it until the sorrow demon didn't feel like a bag of rocks.

"Why did you want me to come back, Cori?" Ethan asked in a low tone. He was still standing like an at-ease soldier.

Cori stepped forward and grabbed the bars to Vince's old cell for support. "Because somewhere between losing a lover and gaining a demon parasite, I saw you. Somewhere between chocolate puffs and worm heart, I admitted to myself that I wanted you. Somewhere between that goodbye kiss and the door closing on the truck, I realized I was in love with you."

She waited a long time for his response. She looked over at him. His eyes were closed, and he was concentrating on his breathing.

"I love you," she repeated, in case he hadn't grasped the extent of her words.

He looked up at her and nodded. "I've been waiting to hear that for a while now."

"I'm so sorry, Ethan. I screwed up." She backed away from the bars and faced him. "I shouldn't have competed. I didn't really think I could win. I just thought I would try to make Danato look good. I tried to throw the shield off, but it was stuck."

Ethan took two long steps to her and crushed her in an embrace. "Don't apologize for winning."

"It was my stupid, dumb luck," she said, muffled by his shoulder.

He rubbed her back. "Lady Luck does have your number, that's for sure."

She detected humor in his voice and she looked up. A strange quirk of a smile was seeping into his face. "You did want to come back to me, didn't you?" she asked, realizing that he had not said "I love you" back to her yet.

He looked down at her. His eyes flickered over her face. He placed his hands on either side of her face. "Say it again, so I know I'm not imagining it."

She wondered what he meant, but the anticipation in his eyes told her the answer. "I love you," she whispered.

He took a deep breath and licked his lips. His eyes showed just a hint of moisture. "One more time, please."

Cori smiled, but she understood how long he had been waiting to have his feelings reciprocated, if indeed he still had those feelings. "I love you, Ethan." She added his name, so there would be no mistaking who she meant.

He threw his head back, blinking away that excess moisture, and took in a few rapid breaths to prepare for what Cori hoped would be another long, sensuous kiss. His head dipped down and his hands pulled her forward. She closed her eyes and parted her lips.

His warm lips descended onto her. With firm pressure, he offered a sincere, emotionally loaded smooch to her forehead. He backed away, slipping from her arms before she could object. After two or three backwards steps, he turned and ran out of the room.

She stood there waiting for her kiss, waiting for her "I love you," and waiting for an explanation.

46

AFTER A GOOD DEAL of time waiting for Ethan, Cori headed back home. She was probably supposed to meet and greet with the judges or something, but she didn't have the energy. She also probably should check into the infirmary to get her ribs checked out, but she wasn't in the mood to be poked and prodded.

She made her way back to the main foyer and found her coat. She could hear a commotion from the gym. She wondered what other festivities they had planned for the day.

She zipped up her coat, positioned her scarf, and prepared to head out the main doors to the house. Secretly, she was hoping Ethan was there so he could explain his buffoonery.

"Leaving so soon?"

Turning back, she saw Danato coming from the hallway the gym was in. She smiled a fake smile, but dropped it right away. There was no point in pretending with Danato. He knew her too well to believe her, anyway.

"I'm sorry, Danato. I know I have obligations, but can't I just go home for a little while?"

"Would you like to tell me why you've been crying?"

Once again, she considered saying something evasive, but he had lived every day with her the last eight months. He knew how much she had been missing Ethan. "I told Ethan I loved him."

"That sounds like something to be cheerful about, not tearful."

She shrugged.

"So why aren't you two stashed in a broom closet somewhere?"

Cori smiled. "Aside from that, not being my style... He didn't really reciprocate his feelings for me. At least not in the way that might have led to said broom closet."

"That's too bad. He does love you, though. I know that for a fact."

"I know." Cori nodded with a thin smile. "But now that he isn't going to be able to stay here and be warden, it makes things complicated."

"He can stay here and be warden if he wants. He just has to beat the dragon faster than you did."

Cori tipped her head. "I thought... he can compete? He can beat me. He can stay here and be warden!" She practically jumped at hearing this revelation. The pain in her calves kept her down to earth, though. "We have to tell him. He should do it today before the judges leave."

"Yes, he should, and he is." Danato's face couldn't fully hold back the smile he was trying to hide. "And you're kind of missing it."

Her eyes widened. "He's in there now?"

"Yes, the match just started. You might want to..." Cori ripped off her coat and threw it at Danato on her way to the gym.

Cori sneaked inside and skirted behind the bleachers to the outskirts where Ethan had watched her compete. Ethan was in the middle of the gym, sword in hand, bare chested, pouring sweat, and breathing hard. He looked unharmed until he turned his back to her. A long red gash peeled the skin on his back. The blood had stained his jeans down to the thigh.

He looked tired, but he was still fighting with all his might.

She stood on the sidelines, feeling the same angst he must have felt watching her. She caught sight of Belus, and he gave her a nod. She sneaked over as if library silence was necessary in a room with a screeching dragon. "Is he doing well?" She kneeled on one knee to save his neck from craning to look at her.

"He lost his shield, but his blows are keeping it at bay." Belus looked back at her legs. "How are you doing?"

She looked over at him with the same stuttered shock that she'd had when he approached her before the battle. "Good, err... two slashes on the calves, a puncture on the left thigh, an irritating, long cut on my left arm, and maybe a broken rib or two," she reported dutifully.

Belus nodded, looking over each wound as she mentioned it, as if he were going to catalogue them in a report. When he said nothing more, she found herself watching him, still waiting for that final statement. The one that would make everything okay.

When he caught her staring, he looked back at her. "What is it?"

She opened her mouth, but nothing came out. There was nothing she could say that wouldn't sound needy. "Thank you." She finally blurted out that.

"You did good today, kid." He turned away even as he said it, which was good, since the smile that fastened itself to her face would have made him roll his eyes.

Ethan slid to a stop on his knees just after being batted by the beast. The dragon came after him again, playing the part of the cat. His paw raised, prepared to flatten him to the floor. Ethan had his back to the animal. Cori's mouth opened to yell, "*Watch out!*" but Belus's hand latched onto hers.

She shut her mouth. Ethan saw her on the sidelines. She frantically nodded to look behind him. He gave her a nod and winked.

The paw descended onto Ethan's back, just as his sword ejected from under his arm. The pointed sword buried between the creature's toe pads. He groaned in pain and pulled back his paw.

"Oh, that poor thing," Cori said.

Belus arched a brow at her concern.

The crowd started to applaud and rally, just as they had for her triumph.

"Did he do it? Is he warden?"

Belus checked the clock. "He did it in less time. That should do it."

Cori smiled and clapped her hands together. The crowd had already huddled around him. She tried to see him through the people, but she couldn't.

"You can go see him, Cori," Belus said. "Go congratulate him."

She got up from her knees and rushed into the crowd. She couldn't see him until she was right on top of him. He was genuflecting in the same place he had been for the final blow. He was leaning over his sword and his one knee. The gash on his back was extensive and deep. She wasn't sure he would get away with no stitches.

Everyone had clustered around him, but given his bloody back, no one gave him the physical cajoles they gave her. Most everyone was talking with each other about the excitement of two matches in one day.

She stepped closer. When her feet were in view, he looked up. She put her hand to his cheek. "Are you okay?" she asked.

He took her hand and pulled her down to his knee. As soon as she was in position, sitting on his half lap, he pulled her face to his. His lips latched onto hers. His gentle kiss offered an apology for anything that might have resembled disinterest earlier.

They came up for air, only to mark the moment with a look of liberation.

He pulled her in again, this time for a deeper, more insistent kiss. The noise of the crowd fell to a distant hum. They were the only ones in the room at that moment.

Cori felt her heart race; the longevity of the kiss reminded her of how much more she wanted to share with Ethan. Their kissing slowed in pace, but increased in depth.

She got the sense that the crowd had trickled away from them. She even heard a couple of distant "ahems" as Danato tried to break up their make-out session. They both ignored him. They had waited far too long to let a little thing like propriety get in their way.

As lip-locked as they were, in the end, it only took three words to separate them. "It's a tie," said one of the judges.

Their hungry lips, suddenly satisfied, parted. They joined the rest of the baffled faces: Danato, Belus, and the judges.

"What?" they both said together.

"His written score was lower than hers. They tied," one judge explained.

"You've got to be kidding me," Ethan said. "That's not possible. I studied forever on that."

"No mistake, she beat out the last four wardens on her written score," the judge concluded with certainty

"No freaking way."

"Hey!" Cori said, once again annoyed that no one could believe her score.

47

The argument on the topic of who beat whom, and how the problem should be rectified, continued back in Danato's office. Danato had mostly stayed out of the argument. The judges bickered about the necessity of knowledge over strength and vice versa until their faces were red with anger. Not one could find an argument that satisfied rejecting one candidate or the other.

Ethan arrived late into the meeting. As he entered, Danato gave him a nod and raised his brow in question to his injuries. Ethan nodded back. The nurses had no doubt patched up his back and given him the appropriate antibiotics. His pink shirt was back on, covering any other bruises and scratches that he might have sustained in the fight.

Ethan looked over at the judges, who were standing in the office's corner by the water cooler and fervently gesturing their points. He grimaced at Danato. Danato rolled his eyes back in testimony to the scene.

Ethan sat on the second chair in front of the desk beside Cori. She looked over at him with a half-smile. She looked concerned, but she said nothing. Her attention shifted to her thigh.

Belus was offering first aid to her injuries. He had already stitched up the cuts on her calves. Danato was surprised to see him injecting her thigh wound with Lidocaine before starting his stitches. Danato was unfamiliar with any time Belus had numbed a wound prior to stitching. Either the wound was deep, or he was taking pity on Cori. A rare gift indeed.

He watched Cori's hand drift down off the arm of her chair to hang off to the side. Ethan's hand did the same, and they interlaced their fingers. She looked back at the judges and then at Ethan.

"I cheated," she said, not taking her eyes from Ethan. "Give Ethan the wardenship."

Danato froze along with the others and looked at her askance. The judges looked at him to answer for this. "That's impossible. I observed the test myself. She was searched for cheat sheets prior to entering the room."

The judges turned to her. "It is impossible to cheat," one judge said. "The test is twenty-eight pages. You couldn't possibly memorize all the answers in order. Where would you get a copy of the test? We don't keep any here."

"I used Cleos." Cori looked at Danato. She knew he wouldn't approve. "He told me what to study, what areas to focus on, so I wasn't studying anything that wasn't going to be on the test."

"He told you the answers?" Danato asked, exchanging a look with Belus. Ethan revealed no emotion to the announcement one way or another. *Smart man.*

"No, he didn't even tell me the specific questions. He just told me what areas to focus on."

A long pause filled the room as everyone thought about that. Danato looked at the judges and shrugged. He didn't see that as cheating. Apparently, neither did they, because they erupted into another debate.

"That's not cheating, that's just a study guide," said one judge.

"No more cheating than a current warden offering his best knowledge to the successor. Danato could have just as easily hinted unknowingly to Ethan what areas to study harder on."

Danato blocked out the rest of the conversation. He was already bored with it. He knew in the end that the three judges would concede to whomever his primary choice was. After all, he had been running this prison for too damn long not to have that privilege.

Cori leaned back in her chair. Sadness crept into her face and her shoulder sagged a little more. Ethan squeezed her hand, but she didn't look up. He sat back with the same sad expression darkening his eyes.

Danato admired the remarkable change in them. Neither one was arguing one way or the other. They had all but given up the fight and resigned themselves to whatever lay ahead. He wasn't sure he was happy about that, but at least they weren't tearing each other's heads off.

"You two," he said in a low tone so he didn't disturb the judges. "Step outside with me."

Ethan slipped out the office door while Danato waited for Belus to finish his bandage on Cori's leg. Once she was mobile, he directed her out the door. She limped out into the hallway with Ethan.

As Danato stepped out with them, he shut the door behind them. The babbling of the judges was instantly cut off, without a murmur of sound to hint at their presence. He looked over his two potential wardens carefully.

Ethan's chin lifted, and his hands clasped in front of him. He was prepared for whatever reaming they were about to receive. Danato had noticed over time that Ethan had become immune to his particular anger, but he'd also developed a loyal respect that was far more impressive than emotional control.

Cori, on the other hand, slumped back into the back wall and crossed her arms. He had grown to love her as a daughter, and over the last months alone with her, that relationship had only grown. She still cowered at his angry rebukes, but their new bond made it almost impossible for him to use it against her.

"What do you two want?" He looked between them. They exchanged a look. "This decision will be made yet tonight. What do you want?"

"I want Ethan to stay," Cori said.

He looked at Ethan, who nodded. "I want to stay."

"Do you want to be warden, though?" Danato asked sternly. He turned his gaze on Cori. "And do you want to continue just being a worker bee?"

Ethan looked at Cori. He silently asked that same question. She looked at Ethan. "I just want us to be together. If that means being a peon, so be it."

Ethan's face shrank, and he shook his head. "If this is important to you, you shouldn't give it up. Maybe I can visit more often."

"No!" Cori looked away from both of them. "I don't want to be here alone." Even as she said it, she looked wide-eyed at Danato. "I love you and Belus, but it's not the same without Ethan."

Danato smiled. "I know, sweetheart. Are you willing to give Ethan the warden position so you can be together?"

She nodded. "Can you make that happen?"

"I tend to get my way in the end." He winked at her and she rushed forward to hug him in a tight embrace that she immediately retreated from in pain. She laughed at her self-punishment and instead gave him a kiss on the cheek.

"You understand, though. You are both going to be here for the remainder of your lives." They looked at him, seemingly not understanding why he was going over the same speech he had on their first meeting. "Ethan, Cori, this thing between you. I see it and I know it's real, but this isn't spring break. This isn't the kind of place you want to explore your relationship to see where it goes. I strongly urge you both to consider the commitment you're making." When neither responded, he added, "This job is forever. Your relationship needs to be forever. Or at the very least, strong enough to be right next to each other if it isn't."

Cori and Ethan looked at each other a moment as if a silent conversation were taking place. Their hands crept back to each other, embracing the way their bodies couldn't. They both turned and nodded at him.

"Okay." Danato nodded. He went back to the office door, and they fell in line behind him. "You know," and he turned back around so suddenly that Cori jumped, "this may take a while. There's a bit of social maneuvering involved here. You two should really get back to the house and rest. You both look a little tired." He smiled at them and went back into the office, closing the door on them.

C ORI AND ETHAN MADE it to the front door before anticipation drove them into each other's arms and a heated lip lock. They fell through the door and relinquished their embrace so they could remove their coats. She ripped hers off and threw it to the floor. The house would surely understand that hormones trumped cleanliness.

Ethan groaned and retreated away from her as he shrugged out of his. "Shit, that hurts."

Cori helped him shift the sleeves down and off his arms. "How bad is it?" She lifted the back of his shirt and frowned. "Oh, Ethan, I don't know if we should do this right now. You're already—"

Ethan grabbed her and pulled her around to face him. "I have waited long enough for you, Cori." He pushed her back into the kitchen and up against the counter. "I will not wait another second." He grabbed her face and kissed her. He pressed against her, introducing her to exactly what he had waited so long to offer her.

He grabbed her thighs and lifted her onto the counter. She yelped as she felt the cut on her thigh explode with fresh pain. He pulled away to look at her. His lustful eyes sobered and he frowned at her wound. "Shit, Cori. I'm sorry. You're too sore for this, aren't you?"

She shook her head. "No, I can do it."

"Cori," he whispered.

"I can!"

"I don't want to hurt you." He touched her cheek, and she leaned into it, kissing his palm. She reached for his waistband and tugged him closer. "I won't do this, if it's going to hurt—ouch!" He yelped as she bit his thumb. She had meant it to be playful, but she underestimated her enthusiasm.

"Sorry, sorry, sorry." She kissed his finger, and then, for an extra incentive, she wrapped her lips around it, drawing it into her mouth suggestively.

Ethan closed his eyes and shook his head. "You are killing me here."

"Then keep going," she panted. "I know you want me."

"More than anything." He wrapped his arms around her and pulled her back against him. She instinctively wrapped her legs around him, pressing her calves against him. She gasped at the stinging pain from her wounds.

"Nope." Ethan pulled away.

"Wait!" She grabbed on tight and slid off the counter after him, clinging to his chest like a monkey.

"Cori, stop. I don't want any part of this experience to be painful to you. I love you and I want our first time together to be special."

"Ethan..." Cori stared into his resolute eyes and sighed. She released her legs, and he helped her down to the floor. "I want it to be special, too."

"Don't pout." He smirked at her and kissed her. She tried to deepen the kiss, but he backed away and leaned on the fridge. She leaned against the sink and crossed her arms, trading in her out for a glare. "Glare all you want, sweetness. It won't change my mind."

Cori stared at him, looking over his handsome features. As frustrating as it was to have her desires put on ice, she was glad that he was being considerate of her comfort. Not that she didn't fully intend to get her way before the day was through.

"You did good today." He stared back at her. "You never cease to amaze me. Are you sure you're okay with me being the warden?"

Cori shrugged. "I never really expected to get it. I just wanted to try, and frankly, after you left, it took all the fun out of it." She bit back her lip and moved to lean on the stove, closer to him. "Can I ask you something?"

"Of course."

"Have you thought about the future?"

"As warden? I try not to. It still seems a little daunting to me."

She cleared her throat. "No, I mean us." She bit her nail.

"I've thought about you and I a lot, Cori. More than you'll ever know."

She chuckled. "I don't mean sex, Ethan. Danato made a good point. This..." She motioned between them. "...needs to be more than a fling."

Ethan's eyes drifted from her. "Is that what you think this is?"

"No, of course not, but..." She moved to him and touched his chest. "This isn't a normal situation. I mean, we're committing to a life together before we've committed to each other."

He looked at her, his eyes dimming with his mood. "Are you having second thoughts?"

"What? No, I just mean that being warden and being with me doesn't have to be a package deal."

"Are you kidding me with this, right now?" Ethan snapped, and straightened his stance. "I just fought a dragon to stay with you. I'm here for *you*! Fuck the job!"

Cori backed away from him, raising her hands in surrender. "I'm not—I'm trying to tell you that I'm okay with it."

"Okay, with what?"

"Forever!" she yelled. He stared at her, his eyes narrowed in confusion. She moved toward him again, but didn't touch him. "I love you, Ethan," she whispered. "And I just came to the realization today that I want to spend the rest of my life with you, but I wasn't sure if you were at that point yet."

He rolled his eyes and walked away. She didn't bother following him.

"I'm sorry if I'm not saying this right," she continued to defend her statement. "I just know that some men don't like being tied down."

Ethan scoffed and reached into his coat pocket. "Some men? I am not *some men*." He dug around in the pocket until he found what he wanted and pulled it out.

A glove.

He brought the glove over and pulled out a small black box he had stuffed into it. The type of hinged black box that usually held jewelry.

He set the box on the island and crossed his arms. Cori eyed the little cube before turning her attention back to him. "What's that?"

"The tenth ring. I told you I had it." She looked back at the box. She reached out for it, but Ethan snagged it away faster than the last Twinkie. She stared at him in shock. "That's not yours yet." His face didn't show a glimmer of amusement. "I just wanted you to know I have it." He slipped the box in his back pocket. "I just wanted you to know that I have thought about our future. And no, not just the sex."

Cori gulped and looked him over. "Ethan—"

"You told me to leave, and I did. You wanted me to make sure that I would still choose you, and I do."

Cori smiled and moved to him. "You chose me over the whole world?"

"You are my world," he leaned in and kissed her. She wrapped her hands around him, being careful not to grip him too tightly. They parted, and he smiled at her. "Maybe we can try this again... a little slower."

49

DANATO STARED AT THE judges battling out the logistics of the testing. He had already told them he was choosing Ethan as his replacement, but they didn't seem to care about that anymore. It had more or less turned into a debate on brains versus brawn.

Belus had taken up the chair in front of his desk to watch the regressive argument. He turned to Danato and shook his head. "This is all your fault, you know?"

"What is my fault?" Danato asked.

"Everything from day one leading up to this..." Belus twirled his finger in the air. "...bullshit."

"How is this..." Danato retorted with another finger twirl. "...my fault?"

"You were supposed to bring back one person for the warden job. One, not two."

Danato nodded and grimaced. "I suppose it's too late to send one back."

"Yeah, little bit." Belus smiled, but it faded fast. He glanced at the judges and leaned forward in his chair.

"Since we're on the subject of things that are too late to take back..." Belus swallowed. "I was wondering when you plan to tell them about Olivia."

Danato's chin jutted forward, and he glanced at their squabbling guests. They were thoroughly occupied with their argument and wouldn't be listening in, but he couldn't help but think that Belus had intended to have an audience for this conversation. It was a little underhanded for him, but nonetheless clever.

"Gentlemen!" Danato barked to interrupt their quarrel. "Get out." They each looked from Danato to Belus and back again before shuffling out the door. Once they were alone, Danato gave his friend a civil smile. "Tell them about what exactly?" He shrugged, pretending to be indifferent to the topic.

"Ethan and Cori are officially part of this prison now. They've proved their loyalty and I think they deserve our honesty. They should be told about *all* the dangers in this prison."

Danato furrowed his brow. He wasn't sure why Belus was suddenly doubting his ability to train his staff, but he was more than happy to answer for it. "I think you and I have done an excellent job detailing the dangers in this prison. As we will continue to do in the future to keep them vigilant."

"That's not what I mean. I don't want to limit their knowledge just because the facts are personal. I know how hard it is for you to talk about her, but—"

"You do?" Danato raised his brow. "You know?" He bit back his anger to keep his volume low. "I'm sure that you have no idea what I feel."

Belus's jaw clenched, and he took a breath. "I'm not going to compare pain with you, Danato. We've been through this. There are no winners in that competition."

"No, there aren't, so let's just drop it." Belus looked away, but Danato could tell that he was nowhere near done making his point. Belus wasn't an easy man to anger, but the topic of Olivia always brought out the worst in both of them.

"I'm just saying," Belus said, maintaining a firm grip on his diplomatic tone. "History has a tendency to repeat itself. Especially when we are ignorant of it."

"Nothing like that will ever happen again."

"You're sure of that?" Belus asked.

"Yes," Danato assured him, "I won't let it."

"It may not be something you can stop. You know Cori doesn't adhere to the rules as well as Ethan. I just don't want to see her get hurt, because you neglected to warn her."

"They both know about the eight dead guards. One more body won't make the difference in their adherence to the rules."

"It will make a difference in how they view this place... and in how they view us."

Danato leaned back in his chair. He was finally seeing the purpose of this discussion. He didn't like it any better, but he couldn't help but chuckle at Belus. "What do you want me to do? Tell them that I'm not the good guy. I think they kind of figured that out when I bought them off a slave auction."

"I'm just going to say this, because it needs to be said, and it's my job to do so. I'm glad that Cori passed her test today, but you and I both know Ethan is the right choice for this job. Cori is too impetuous; she needs to understand that her mistakes can have consequences that don't involve potted plants."

Danato stared at him, waiting for his temper to simmer down before he broke his desk... again.

"Cori needs to know the truth about Olivia," Belus said. "Not just so she doesn't make the same mistakes, but so she starts to take the rules more seriously."

Danato considered his point, but ultimately he didn't agree. The only purpose that bedtime story served was to scare her into obedience. If worse came to worst, he could use that tactic, but not after everything she had done to earn her place in the competition. And certainly not after he had finally gained her trust and friendship.

"I appreciate your concerns, Belus, and I would be happy to relinquish the continuation of her training to you if you think you know best. However, the details of my wife's death are not a topic I wish to discuss with anyone. Not now. Not ever."

FELICIA JEDLICKA
LOVERS & LIARS
Book 3
THE WARDEN

LOVERS AND LIARS

Sneak Peek

ETHAN APPROACHED DUKE WITHOUT his usual smile. Duke, however, had a broad one for him. "Hey, boss man." He pulled Ethan's outstretched hand into a one-armed manly slap hug. "What brings you to the roof without a coat?" Duke looked him over, slowly losing his smile as he did.

Ethan was in his usual black t-shirt and black cargo pants, just like the other guards. He had never seen a reason to distinguish himself, even after receiving his title. Duke was bundled to the nines with a hooded jacket, ski mask, gloves, and something that looked like chaps. The fall season wasn't as cold as the winter, but it was still too damn cold to be stepping outside without the proper attire.

"Could I have you step away from your post for a bit?" Ethan said, trying to smile, but failing.

"Sure thing, boss," Duke said, propping his weapon on his shoulder. Ethan didn't like that he called him "boss." It made him feel separate from him, but since Duke wasn't the type to give up a nickname, Ethan never requested he stop. Somehow, asking him to stop calling him "boss" seemed bossy.

They stepped back into the stairwell, and Ethan stopped at the first landing. Duke must have realized the seriousness of the situation, because he gripped his weapon tightly with both hands. Ethan could see the furrow in his brow, even through the ski mask.

"Why the long face?"

"I have a job for you to do."

Duke slapped his shoulder and guffawed. "Is that all? You know I ain't too proud to do my job." His Texan accent laced his words with a friendliness that couldn't be beat by any other burr. "What can I do for y'all?"

"I need you to arrest my wife," Ethan said.

Thank you so much for reading. I hope you enjoyed the ride and if you aren't getting off here, I encourage you to sign up for my newsletter so I can return your generosity with new release updates and special offers.

Sign-Up

You can also find me on Facebook or visit my website. Keep reading!

Website

Facebook

AUTHOR

A s a Nebraska native, and a small-town girl at that, I have very little to occupy my time beyond imagining a world outside of my own reality. By the grace of God and the seat of my pants, I have kept my waning attention span on the task of becoming an author.

So here I am, an indie author, peddling my words in cyberspace and enduring my comeuppances with an unwavering determination. I may not be a professional, and I certainly am not perfect, but if you've made it this far, you have to admit, this smartass yokel does spin quite a yarn.

From the self-inflicted sweatshop conditions of my unairconditioned childhood home, to the arthritis reaping positions of a sedentary lifestyle, I bring to you: my sarcasm, my oddity, and my heart. Take it with a grain of salt or a teaspoon of sugar, but take it for what it is: a story born of the mind, translated to paper, and gifted to you.

I thank you for your readership and even more for your support. Please recommend this book to your friends and family via any social media that you use. Word of mouth is still the best advertising and is greatly appreciated.

Most importantly, keep reading. I'll keep writing.